# CLASS SIX and the NITS of DOOM

## SALLY PRUE

*Illustrated by*
## KELLY CANBY

A & C BLACK

First published 2014 by A & C Black,
an imprint of Bloomsbury Publishing Plc
50 Bedford Square
London WC1B 3DP
Bloomsbury is a registered trademark of Bloomsbury Publishing Plc

www.bloomsbury.com

ISBN  978 1 4729 0459 1

A CIP catalogue for this book is available from the British Library.

Printed and bound by CPI Group (UK) Ltd, Croydon CR0 4YY

1 3 5 7 9 10 8 6 4 2

# CHAPTER ONE

It was the first day back at school after the summer holidays and the playground was full of excited children. Class Three were hopping up and down inside their enormous new school coats, and Classes Four and Five were charging about shouting WE WENT TO THE SEASIDE AND EVERYWHERE SMELLED OF EGGIES! or else huddled in groups comparing hair clips.

But just inside the school gate there was another group of children. They were a bit bigger than the others, but they weren't excited or running about. These children had pale faces, and eyes that glittered with fear. From time to time a trembling child crept in through the school gate to join them, but not one of them took a single step nearer the school than was absolutely necessary.

One boy was just looking at his watch, as if in some forlorn hope that the hands would start going backwards, when from a long way off there came a rattling. It came closer and closer until a small car came into view. Its bumper was tied on with string, its wings were patched with duct tape, and it was covered in grime and rust.

'Here comes Rodney,' said the boy with the watch.

The car stopped by the school gate and one of the doors flapped open. Out of the opening came a large foot. And then another.

All the children, their faces blue with terror, stared at the boy who got out of the car.

Rodney waved a big hand at them.

'I span round really fast fifty-three times last night,' he said, proudly. 'And I *still* wasn't sick!'

And then he shouldered his way through the group of children by the gate and strolled happily down towards the school building.

There was a long pause as the children watched Rodney walk away.

'He's not scared,' said Jack, at last.

'Of course he's not,' said Serise grumpily. 'He's too stupid to be scared. I bet Rodney's too stupid to be scared of a charging bull, even. Or a runaway

4

double-decker bus. Or a shark jumping out of the canal with its jaws wide open.'

'Or a witch,' said Emily, in a small voice.

Everyone froze. Then they all nodded sadly.

'The bell will be going soon.' Anil looked at his watch again. 'And then we'll *have* to go in, won't we.'

Emily started crying.

'Four minutes, exactly,' went on Anil. 'Three minutes fifty-five seconds. Three minutes fifty—'

Slacker Punchkin put a flabby arm absent-mindedly round Anil's neck and tried to strangle him.

'The trouble with Rodney is that he doesn't believe there's any such thing as witches,' Slacker said. 'He's just like a grown-up that way.'

'Yes,' said Serise scornfully. 'Stupid.'

'I mean, even my dad said it was silly to worry about a witch,' went on Slacker.

Winsome rescued Anil. 'Perhaps it *is* silly.'

Emily sniffed sadly. 'But we've all seen it,' she said. 'Magic, all over the whole school. And we saw how peculiar last year's Year Six went.'

'I suppose so,' agreed Winsome, frowning. 'But then we never heard any of them actually say *my class teacher Miss Broom is a witch*, did we?'

'That's true,' said Jack, perking up a bit.

Serise turned on him with contempt. 'No,' she snapped. 'But I've heard them say *Miss Broom's a winter vest!* and *Miss Broom's a weasel's nostril!*'

Emily started crying again.

'Yes,' agreed Anil. 'Just as if something was stopping them saying the word *witch*. Just as if they were all under some spell which stopped them telling anyone about it.'

Winsome tried to look brave. 'Well, at least year's Year Six all survived, didn't they? I mean, they didn't end up turned into toadstools or piglets or anything.'

There was a short pause.

'Although we never did find out where all those rhinoceroses came from that were out in the playing field that day,' Anil pointed out.

Jack suddenly grinned.

'Hey, it'd be brilliant to be a rhino,' he said. 'If I was a rhino I'd charge right through the Co-op spearing doughnuts on my horn and no one would be able to stop me.'

'Oh yes they would,' snapped Serise. 'Someone would shoot you.'

Anil looked at his watch again. 'It's nearly time for the bell,' he said. 'Ten…nine…'

'No they wouldn't!' said Jack. 'Rhinos have armour-plated skin, don't they? And anyway they're really rare so you're not allowed to shoot them, not even if they charge right into car parks and start crushing all the cars with their enormous great feet, and—'

'…two…one…'

**BRRRRRRRRRRRRRRRRRRRRRRRRRRRRRRRRIIIIIII
IIIIIIIIIIIIIIIIINNNNNNNNNNNNNNNGGGGG
GGGGGGGGGGGGGGGGGG!!!!!!!!!!!!!!**

All the children jumped several centimetres into the air and clutched at each other in terror, and several of them screamed.

Slacker Punchkin shook his head sadly.

'That's it,' he said. 'There's no escape, now. We're doomed.'

Emily began jumping up and down.

'I don't want to die I don't want to die I don't want to die!' she shrieked, but Winsome put her arm round her.

'You'll be all right,' Winsome said. 'Miss Broom would be sent to prison if she did anything bad to us. You know that really. Come on.'

The rest of Class Six looked at each other, and the sound of their knocking knees could be heard even above the chattering of all the other classes as they filed into school.

And then Class Six sighed, and they slowly and reluctantly began to trudge down the school path towards their new classroom.

And towards their new teacher, Miss Broom.

The witch.

# CHAPTER TWO

Miss Broom didn't actually look that much like a witch. Instead of being as tall as a drainpipe and as thin as a stick insect she was shortish and had big bosoms. Her face wasn't green, her teeth weren't black, and her nose wasn't warty, either. She didn't even have a beard.

'I expect she shaves it off every morning,' whispered Serise to Jack, behind her hand.

Miss Broom turned to the whiteboard and wrote:

*Miss Wilhelmina Broom*

in big letters, and Class Six took the opportunity to have a good look at her back. She showed no signs of having a tail, and her hair wasn't witchy,

miss Wilhelmina Broom

either: it was bouncy and sand-coloured instead of all black and jagged.

It was only her eyes, really, that gave the game away. They were shining amber like a tiger's, and when you looked into them, instead of seeing your own reflection, you might see anything: a full moon rising over a graveyard; a flock of fanged bats; a cauldron simmering by candlelight; a knitted tea cosy—

'*A knitted tea-cosy?*' Anil had echoed incredulously, earlier, when Class Six had been comparing notes. 'Are you *sure*, Emily?'

'I suppose it might have been a woolly hat,' Emily had admitted timidly.

9

'You mean, like a football hat?' Jack had said. 'Hey, what colour?'

Emily had looked even unhappier.

'United's colours,' she'd whispered.

Everyone had exchanged appalled glances, and Anil had shaken his head.

'Being a witch is one thing,' he'd said, trying to be fair. 'I mean, you probably can't help being a witch, any more than I can help being really good at maths. But supporting *United*...'

And that had been the moment when Class Six had really truly and utterly believed that they were doomed.

Miss Broom turned back from the whiteboard and smiled at all the children. It was a strange, creepy sort of smile that made everyone feel as if spiders were running down their backs towards their underpants, but at least Miss Broom didn't appear to have fangs.

'Well, aren't you sitting nice and quietly,' said Miss Broom. 'Now, let's find out all your names.'

And she began to call the register.

Six small owls emerged from a hole in the front of her desk while she was reading out the names. They flew low over the children's heads and perched along the top of the bookshelves. The owls had bright amber eyes just like Miss Broom, but the pictures in their enormous eyes showed beetles and bats and mice.

Half-eaten beetles and bats and mice.

★ ★ ★

Class Six tottered pale-faced out into the playground at break time and stood in a trembling group, too shattered even to think about playing. They were too shattered to speak, too. They stood, completely silent except for a strange slurping, crunching sound behind them like the turning of a badly rusted washing machine.

But that was only Slacker Punchkin eating his breaktime snack of three meat pasties, so they were used to it.

At last Winsome took a deep brave breath.

'At least we're alive,' she said.

'We are for now,' said Serise dourly. 'But who knows if we'll be alive by lunch time. We've been at School Assembly ever since registration. By lunch time Miss Broom might have turned us into gerbils.'

'Lamp posts.'

'Pies.'

'Zombies. Or mummies.'

'Not mummies,' said Slacker, spraying Class Six with pie crumbs. 'She'd never find enough bandages to wrap me up.'

Rodney was looking at them as if they were mad. 'That's stupid. There's no such things as witches. You all know that. Miss Broom's just an ordinary boring old teacher.'

And now it was Anil's turn to stare at Rodney as if *he* was mad. But that was fair enough.

'*What?*' Anil said. 'So where do you think all those owls came from? And that shower of bus tickets?'

'The owls came out of a hole in her desk,' Rodney answered. 'You don't have to be a witch to keep pets, do you? My nan's got a ferret. And the bus tickets probably...' He frowned for a moment, thinking hard, and then his face brightened. 'The bus tickets probably came off a bus!' he finished up, triumphantly.

'And where do you suppose the bus tickets all went, Rodney?' asked Winsome, quite kindly. 'I mean, once they'd stopped flying round the classroom like jet-powered moths and singing that really high-pitched little song about always trusting Miss Broom and always doing as we were told?'

Rodney shrugged. 'That was just an optical delusion.'

'And so were all the gibbons,' said Serise scathingly. '*And* the thunder and lightning coming out of the art cupboard.'

Rodney pulled up two bunches of scraggy weeds from the flowerbed behind him, rolled them up carefully, and stuck them in his ears.

That was the sort of thing he did all the time. No one knew why. Least of all Rodney.

'There's no such thing as witches,' he said stubbornly. 'And I bet I can prove it, too. All we have to do is make Miss Broom really annoyed, and if we don't get turned into toadstools then we'll *know* she's not a witch.'

The bell went for the end of break. Jack screamed and jumped so violently he ended up with his arms and legs wrapped round one of the netball posts.

'That's it,' said Serise grimly. 'We are *so* going to be dead.'

'Well, at least if Rodney goes and annoys Miss Broom then he'll be dead first,' pointed out Anil, as they went to line up. 'That's something.'

But Winsome, who was very kind and sensible, pulled the bunches of weeds out of Rodney's ear holes.

'I think you'd best be good, Rodney,' she said.

'No,' said Jack, flapping his fingers between horror and a sort of dreadful delight. 'Go on, Rodney! You prove to us all that Miss Broom is just an ordinary human and not a witch, and that all those sardines that Emily found in her drawer had swum there by themselves during the holidays.'

Rodney smiled happily. Not only was he easily the stupidest person in the class, he was probably the most obstinate, too. *And* the least able to recognise a really, really bad idea when he heard one.

'All right, then,' he said, and led the way back to class.

Miss Broom wasn't in the classroom when Class Six arrived. The children looked round anxiously, checking for sharks in the sink and ghosts hanging from the coat hooks, but everything looked more or less normal. Even Emily's drawer, once she'd bribed Slacker to open it for her by promising him her pudding at lunch time, proved to contain nothing more than her pencil case and some exercise books.

'I think there's still a smell of fish, though,' she said, sniffing cautiously.

Slacker Punchkin gave Emily's English book a big fat lick.

'No taste, though,' he reported, with regret.

Jack was whispering excitedly to Rodney. 'What are you going to do to prove Miss Broom's not a witch?' he asked. 'What are you going to do? Hey? What are you going to do?'

Rodney frowned and began twisting at one of his ears. He always did that when he tried thinking. The others had decided his brain must be clockwork, and needed winding up to make it work.

'She *can't* be a witch,' he said. 'There's no such thing as witches.'

Anil clutched at his hair in disbelief.

'Then what about all those spider webs in the rafters?' he yelped. 'The ones with our names woven into them? And what about when all our chairs turned into ponies and carried us round the classroom so we were sitting in alphabetical order?'

'What about that lizard playing *Magic Moments* on all those cucumbers that grew out of the bottom of the whiteboard?' asked Winsome.

Rodney shrugged.

'Like I said, those were just sceptical illusions,' he said. 'Anyway, if Miss Broom was a witch she'd have a broomstick, wouldn't she? And she comes to school on a bicycle.'

'Yes, she does,' agreed Anil. 'A bicycle which goes along by itself without being pedalled. And has ears.'

'Anyway, you don't know she hasn't got a broom,' pointed out Slacker Punchkin. 'She could have one at home. Or hidden somewhere.'

Everyone looked around the classroom.

'It could be in that big cupboard that's got DANGER written on the door,' said Jack. 'Hey, look, the door's not closed properly. That bit of black material's got caught in it and it's stopping it shutting.'

Class Six stared at the door, and they stared at the DANGER sign. The cupboard was big enough to hold all sorts of things. A bear. A full-sized knight in shining armour.

'A cauldron and a book of spells,' said Emily, shuddering.

Slacker Punchkin looked interested.

'A cauldron?' he echoed. 'In there? Hey, I wonder if Miss Broom's cooking anything?'

'No,' said Winsome quickly. 'She couldn't be. Not in a closed cupboard.'

Rodney heaved a great sigh.

'But there *can't* be a cauldron in the cupboard,' he said. 'Because there's no such thing as magic. Look, I'll show you.'

Before anyone could stop him he went over to the cupboard door and flung it open wide.

And everyone gasped.

Emily had been right. On the floor inside the cupboard was a small but definite cauldron. It was full of stuff that looked like turquoise bubble gum, and it was bubbling away in spite of the fact there was no fire underneath it. The steam that swelled out into the classroom smelled of old plimsolls, peanuts and school dinners.

Emily pointed a trembling finger.

'*Look,*' she whispered.

On a hook on the inside of the door was something like an enormous bat skin.

'A witch's cloak!' gasped Winsome.

'With claws,' said Anil, with a gulp.

Rodney put out a finger to scoop up some of the turquoise gunge from the cauldron, but Winsome ran over and grabbed his arm. 'Don't touch it!' she said. 'That's probably a spell! If you touch that, anything could happen. You could turn into a toad, and then you'd only be able to eat slugs and beetles.'

The others found they'd got up and were moving forward towards the cupboard almost without wanting to, as if their feet had developed minds of their own.

Slacker Punchkin licked his lips.

'I bet slugs are really juicy,' he said, as Winsome tried to get Rodney to come away from the cupboard.

'We'd better close the door and go and sit down,' she said. 'Miss Broom will be here any minute and—'

'Look at that!' squawked Serise.

They all looked, and now their eyes had got used to the gloom inside the cupboard, they could see it. Beyond the shifting turquoise steam that rose from the cauldron there was something hanging up on the back wall of the cupboard.

It was a hat.

The cloak hadn't really looked all that different from the gowns teachers wear in cartoons, but there was no doubt about the hat. It was black, it had a broad rim, and the bit in the middle came up to a point.

'That *proves* it!' breathed Jack. 'That's a real witch's hat. It couldn't possibly be anything else.'

But Rodney only hunched his shoulders.

'It doesn't prove anything,' he said. 'It's probably fancy dress. I expect—'

'Quick!' squeaked Emily. There were footsteps just outside the door. 'She's coming! She's coming!'

Everyone moved fast. Even Slacker Punchkin moved fast, charging across the classroom, scattering tables and chairs as he went. By the time Miss Broom's splendid bosom appeared in the doorway Class Six was sitting, arms folded, looking as innocent as they could.

Except for one of them.

Rodney Wright's clockwork brain just wasn't fast enough for emergencies, and the children saw to their horror that Rodney was still standing in the cupboard doorway winding up his ear.

Miss Broom was walking across the classroom to her desk, and in another couple of seconds she was going to turn round. And then she'd see him. Worse than that, she'd see the open cupboard and know that Class Six had seen the cauldron. And the witch's cloak. And the hat.

Luckily, Anil's brain had a gold-plated hard drive. In the final second before Miss Broom's round bottom plumped down onto her seat he put out a foot and kicked the cupboard door closed.

Everyone in Class Six heard the *click!* as it shut.

And Rodney, who was now locked inside the cupboard, heard it best of all.

# CHAPTER THREE

The whole class froze with horror. Rodney was trapped inside the cupboard. Rodney, who was so stupid he didn't believe in witches even after he'd seen the dancing skeletons in Miss Broom's eyes. Any moment now he might start hammering on the door and then—

'Now,' said Miss Broom, smiling a wide smile that was at least three centimetres wider than any smile Class Six had ever seen before. 'We've welcomed all the sweet and juicy new little Year Threes to the school at assembly, and we've given out all our exercise books, so we'd better get down to some work. Right, then...'

Her bright orange eyes swept the classroom and everyone hunched down as small as they could and tried to be invisible.

'Jack,' said Miss Broom.

The rest of Class Six felt relieved for a second, and then got all anxious again. Jack wasn't as stupid as Rodney, but he wasn't one of the clever ones. Why, he was Rodney's best friend, so that proved it. There was no way he was going to be able to fool a witch.

Jack gulped.

'Yes, Miss Broom?'

'Do you know your nineteen times table, dear?'

A wave of panic and dismay went round Class Six. Nineteen times table? They'd learned up to ten times, and *that* had taken ages and ages. *Nineteen?*

But before Jack could reply, Miss Broom's desk drawer opened all by itself and something came out of it. It was something long and slithery. And scaly. It was the same orange as Miss Broom's eyes, and it had black Xs all the way down its back.

It rippled down onto Miss Broom's lap, and then up over her big bosom to coil round her neck.

Class Six closed their eyes, crossed their fingers, and opened them again. Then they tried it again. But the big orange thing was still there, and it was still most definitely a large fat snake.

'Aargh!' said Emily faintly.

Miss Broom laughed. It was a musical laugh, but it was like icicles falling onto a frozen pond and it sent shivers down everyone's spines.

'There's no need to be worried, Emily, dear,' she said. 'Algernon is going to help us learn our tables.'

Algernon raised his head and stared beadily at Class Six, and Class Six stared back, transfixed.

Winsome suddenly found her mind had gone so misty she couldn't see from one end of a thought to the other. *I'm being hypnotised,* she realised. But then that thought dissolved into mist, too, and she was left staring and staring and staring at Algernon's swaying head.

Algernon opened his mouth. Wider and wider and wider it went. It opened to the size of an orange, and then to the size of a dinner plate, and then to the size of a barrel. All Class Six could do was stare down past his gleaming sickle fangs and into the blackness of his throat.

And then, before Class Six had time to work out what was going on, a flock of poison-green scissor-shapes zoomed out of Algernon's mouth and came flying straight towards them.

The quickest of the children ducked down under their tables, but it was no good. The scissor-shapes swooped and slipped through the air, fast as bats, and in a few seconds they had wrapped themselves round the wrists of everyone in Class Six.

Jack squawked and tried to pull the thing off, but it was no good because the X shape was sinking into his skin. It got fainter and fainter and then quite suddenly it vanished altogether.

Jack looked round and found that all the X shapes had disappeared.

Everyone was frozen, stiff with horror, either on the floor or under a table or hiding behind a chair. They were all afraid to move in case their hands fell off, or began to do things by themselves.

Miss Broom smiled round at them all.

'Well, that was exciting, wasn't it,' she said. 'Now. Let's just make sure it's worked. Anil!'

Anil made a noise like a dying frog. He was clutching his wrist as if he was afraid it was going to fall to pieces.

'What's thirteen times twenty-one, please, Anil?'

'Two hundred and seventy-three,' said Anil, at once.

The others blinked a bit—but then Anil *was* a brain at maths, after all, as he kept telling them.

'Quite right. Good boy. Winsome!'

Winsome's mouth moved, but she didn't seem to be able to make any noise at all.

'What's fifteen times seventeen, please?'

'Two hundred and fifty-five,' said Winsome—and then she clapped her hands to her mouth and looked nearly as horrified as if she'd just spat out a tarantula.

'Excellent, dear. Jack! Twenty-seven times eighty-six?'

Class Six looked at each other with pale faces. Anil and Winsome were the cleverest people in the class, but Jack was much too fidgety to think. Even picking up his pen sometimes took too much concentration for him. So there was no way...

Jack's eyes bulged until he looked even more like a bald gerbil than usual. And then strange sounds began to come out of his mouth.

Incredible, extraordinary, amazing sounds.

*'Two thousand three hundred and twenty-two!'* he squawked.

Class Six gasped. Miss Broom smiled and stroked Algernon's scaly back.

'Marvellous, Algernon,' she said. 'You've done that beautifully, as always. And what a relief to have got our times tables out of the way. Class Six, I think we should say thank you to Algernon, don't you?'

Class Six exchanged glances. They'd never spoken to a snake before, but even so none of them felt the slightest wish to argue with Miss Broom.

'Thank you, Algernon,' they all said.

Algernon bowed his flat head politely, as if in reply, and then he slid back down over Miss Broom's big bosom and back into her desk drawer.

'Algernon's *such* a wonderful creature,' said Miss Broom proudly. 'But I must warn you, dears. He would never hurt you on purpose, of course, but I shouldn't disturb him when he's in his drawer. Because of course he *is* a poisonous snake. I expect you saw his fangs.'

Jack was poking his little finger into his ear and then taking it out and looking at it, as if in hope of finding some trace of his new cleverness. But Miss Broom's words caught his attention.

'Poisonous?' he echoed. 'Really? Wow. Is he an adder, then, Miss Broom?'

Miss Broom gave a tinkly little icicle laugh and twenty-nine shudders juddered down twenty-nine spines.

'An adder?' she echoed. 'Why, of course not, dear. No. Adders are rare and special, but Algernon is even rarer and more special than that.'

'Really, Miss Broom?' asked Anil, who was interested in everything to do with science.

'Really,' Miss Broom told them all, very seriously. 'After all, Algernon helped you all with your times tables, didn't he?'

Winsome jumped as if something had stung her.

'You mean...' she began, and then her voice faded away in amazement.

Miss Broom nodded.

'That's right, Winsome,' she said. 'Algernon is a poisonous snake, but he isn't an adder at all. No. Dear Algernon's a *multiplier.*'

# CHAPTER FOUR

'Well, Class Six,' said Miss Broom. 'We've learned our times tables up to nine hundred and ninety-nine times, and that's enough work for anyone in one morning.'

She gave them all a picture of a vampire in a cobwebby castle to colour in. The only slight problem was that the vampire kept getting up and walking about, which made it hard to keep within the lines.

Class Six worked quietly, occasionally whispering things like *what's fifty-three times fourteen?* and *hey, I'm a genius!* to each other.

The back of Anil's colouring sheet was covered in calculations:

$$\begin{array}{r} 53 \\ \times\,14 \\ \hline 212 \\ 530 \\ \hline 742 \end{array}$$

and things like that. He was the only one who wasn't very pleased.

'Hey, you know those fourteen doughnuts I ate at playtime yesterday?' whispered Slacker. 'That was five thousand seven hundred and forty calories. That's quite a lot, isn't it?'

'Masses,' hissed Serise. 'No wonder you're so—'

—but then there came a noise. It was an odd, unearthly sound, a little like someone sawing a piece of wood.

And it was coming from the cupboard with DANGER written on the door.

Class Six froze. In all the excitement they'd almost forgotten that Rodney was shut up in the cupboard.

'What's he *doing*?' asked Serise, in the smallest possible whisper.

'Perhaps he's fallen into the cauldron and it's turned him into a bear,' squeaked Emily.

'He sounds as if he's in agony,' whispered Jack.

But Winsome sat up in sudden understanding.

'No!' she said. 'I know what it is. It's so dark in there that Rodney's decided it's night time, and he's gone to sleep. He's snoring!'

*Krgggggggggggghhhhhh* came from the cupboard.
*Krggggghhhhhh*

Slacker began coughing to try to cover up the sound.

Miss Broom looked up from where she was reading a huge ancient book with a star drawn on the front.

'Are you all right, Slacker?' she asked.

'Yes, he's fine, miss,' said Winsome, hastily. 'There must be a bit of dust about, I think.'

'Really? How unusual.'

Miss Broom snapped her fingers, and immediately half a dozen pink and blue striped rats emerged from Miss Broom's waste paper basket and began to run round the classroom, whisking any bits of dust into their pouches with their long tufted tails.

'I didn't know rats in this country had pouches,' said Jack, lifting up his feet for the rats to sweep underneath them.

'They don't,' said Winsome.

*Krggggggggghhhhhhhhhhhh*

The whole class burst out coughing this time.

'I think the dust's got right down my throat,' gasped Anil.

'Water, water!' coughed Slacker, dramatically.

Miss Broom blinked her orange eyes, and in their reflection Class Six saw a rocky desert with three vultures perched on the ribcage of some large beast.

*Krggggggggghhhhhhhhhhh*

*Cough! Cough-cough choke cough. COUGH!*

'Oh dear,' said Miss Broom, rather alarmed. 'I've never come across this sort of reaction to a simple times table lesson before.'

'Please, Miss Broom,' said Anil hoarsely. 'There are some big water jugs in the dining room. If we could have some water...'

Miss Broom got up in a hurry.

'Of course,' she said. 'I won't be long, Class Six. Do try to stay alive until I get back!'

And she hurried out of the room.

Class Six stopped coughing and looked at each other.

'Right,' said Winsome, getting up. 'We've got about three minutes to get Rodney out of the cupboard.'

Serise went and banged on the door. 'Rodney!' she called. 'Rodney, you idiot!'

Pause.

Then:

'Mum?' a voice said sleepily. 'Is it daytime?'

Everyone groaned.

'Rodney?' called Winsome. 'Can you hear me?'

'Yes, Mum,' said Rodney's voice through the woodwork. 'But I think my eyes have stopped working. And why is my bed standing up on end?'

Serise rolled her eyes.

'It's no good expecting Rodney to be any help,' she muttered. She tugged sharply on the door handle. Nothing happened, so she tried again. And again.

'I can't shift it at all,' she said. 'It must have a really good lock.'

Behind them, Anil frowned.

'Locked?' he echoed. 'But it can't be locked. Look, there's no keyhole.'

Everyone looked and saw that Anil was quite right.

'But...' said Winsome.

'But...' said Emily.

Anil began walking up and down, his fingers to his forehead in his best mad-professor way.

'So how do you get the door open?' he asked. 'Perhaps you need a magic spell.'

'Well, that old book Miss Broom was reading looked like a spell book,' Jack said. 'She put it back in her drawer.'

'Yes, with Algernon,' snapped Serise. 'Do you feel like putting your hands into Miss Broom's drawer to get it out, Jack?'

Jack didn't.

'Does anyone know any magic words?' asked Emily timidly.

'Abracadabra,' suggested someone.

'Hey presto?'

'Sesame!'

'Please,' suggested Slacker thoughtfully. 'Thank you. And pardon.'

There was a sudden clatter from inside the cupboard, and a voice said: *ouch! Ouch! OUCH!*

'Are you all right?' called Winsome anxiously.

'Yes,' said Rodney.

Emily began jumping up and down as if she was about to wet herself. 'Miss Broom will be back any minute. And then she'll turn us into rats or something. We've got to get him out! We've got to get him out!'

'I don't think she'd turn us *all* into rats,' objected Anil. 'I mean, she'd get into trouble if her *whole* class disappeared. I don't think she could really disappear more than one or two of us.'

Serise snorted.

'Well, that's all right, then, if only one or two of us disappear. Hey, do you remember Wayne Mitchell? Because he disappeared last year, didn't he?'

'Yes,' agreed Winsome. 'But only because he moved to Watford.'

Emily looked more frightened than ever.

Anil was still pacing up and down, scowling. 'There must be some spell or word that opens it. Something special...'

'Oh, I *wish* we had an ordinary teacher!' wailed Emily. 'I wish our teacher was just an ordinary human, and the most exciting thing that ever happened was getting a go on the computer!'

Anil stopped dead.

'*That's it!*' he said.

'That's what?' asked everyone, but Anil was striding up to the door of the cupboard.

'*That's* the magic word,' he said. 'The one that gets you in to almost anything. The one people use all the time even though you're never supposed to use it.'

Jack made a puzzled face.

'Do you mean…*bum*?' he asked.

Anil tutted, and put his hand on the cupboard door. Then he said, in a loud commanding voice:

'PASSWORD!'

And instantly the door swung open.

Rodney had been in the dark so long the daylight dazzled him. He rubbed his knuckles into his eyes.

'Look at the state of him!' said Serise, whisking the witch's hat off his head. It must have fallen there off the coat hook. 'He's all over cobwebs!'

He was all over spiders, too—big juicy-looking ones with a skull-and-crossbones design on their backs—but luckily they seemed to like the light even less than Rodney did, and they quickly wound all the bits of cobweb into balls, stuck their knitting needles under their arms, and scuttled back into the cupboard.

'Quick!' said Emily, doing a little jig of terror. 'I can hear her footsteps. Oh, *quick*!'

Slacker pushed Rodney into the nearest chair, and all the rest of the class threw themselves into their places. Some of them even remembered to start coughing again. When Miss Broom arrived with a tray full of beakers they were all red in the face and breathing hard.

Miss Broom viewed them all, still puzzled, as she began to hand out the beakers of water.

'You all must have some sort of an allergy to...er... to my special methods,' she said, as she went round the classroom. 'Perhaps I shall have to stop using them for the time being.'

Class Six sipped their glasses of water and felt very relieved. Miss Broom was going to stop doing magic for a while, and Rodney had been rescued from the cupboard. They were safe.

For the moment.

★　★　★

There must have been something itchy in the witch's cupboard, though, because Rodney had started scratching and scratching and scratching at his head.

# CHAPTER FIVE

Class Six were so weak with relief that they didn't even have the strength to fight to be first in the queue at lunch time.

The children from the other classes stared at Class Six curiously, but none of them dared come up to ask any questions. They all knew about Miss Broom. Every year, Class Six was the best-behaved class in the whole school—and everyone knew why.

It was terror. Sheer, utter terror.

Unless, of course, it was something even worse...

Class Six stood quietly in line, as dull as cows, grateful simply to be still alive, and the only person who wasn't completely shattered was Rodney Wright. The sleep in the cupboard seemed to have perked him up, because he was quite lively. He kept squiggling and scratching. And scratching. And scratching.

'What was it like in the cupboard?' asked Emily timidly, when they were all sitting down and trying to summon up the energy to eat.

Rodney scratched his head.

'Smelly,' he said. 'And dark. I was a bit worried at first because the luminous grasshoppers had huge teeth, but they left me alone so it was all right.'

'Grasshoppers?' echoed Anil.

'Yeah. They were all sort of oily green and purple. But it was OK, they just sat quietly on their shelf and carried on playing backgammon.'

'I would have screamed and screamed and screamed,' said Emily, with a shiver. 'To be locked up with magic grasshoppers...'

Rodney scratched his head again.

'There's no such thing as magic,' he said.

Everyone in Class Six took in a deep breath to say *WHAT?????* But then they just sighed and started eating their dinners. Rodney had always been really stupid. It wasn't that he couldn't read or write or add up or stuff, it was more that it never occurred to him that he might be wrong. Not even the fact that Miss Broom had orange eyes that showed pictures of skulls and vampire bats had made the slightest difference to his belief that there was no such thing as witches.

'The only *scary* thing,' Rodney went on, talking through a mouthful of lettuce, 'was when Miss Broom's hat fell down over my head. It smelled of compost and ferret poo.'

'Yuk!' said Jack.

'Ew!' said Serise. 'That is really *disgusting*. I mean, even if Miss Broom *is* a watch she could still keep her clothes clean, couldn't—'

Serise broke off as she realised that the others were all staring at her. 'What?' she snapped.

'What did you just say, Serise?' asked Winsome quietly.

Serise scowled. 'I said, that even if Miss Broom *is* a watch, then at least—hey, what are you lot looking at?'

'She said *watch*!' squawked Jack, pointing a wavering finger. 'She said Miss Broom is a *watch*!'

'No, I didn't!' snapped Serise. 'Don't be silly. I said she was a *watch*!'

Everyone had gone completely still.

Slacker frowned. 'Say it again.'

Serise began to look defensive.

'Miss Broom is a…is a…is a… *WATCH*!' she said. And then she clapped her hands to her mouth and went all cross-eyed.

Anil took a deep breath.

'Miss Broom is a-a-a *wicket*!' he said. 'I mean, she's a wer-wer-wer-*wick*!'

Class Six looked at each other wildly, and then they all tried.

'Miss Broom is a *wish*!' said Winsome.

'Miss Broom... Miss Broom... Miss Broom is a *with*!' said Slacker.

'Miss Broom,' said Jack, making a great effort. 'Miss Broom is a wer-wer-wer...a wer-wer-wer...a wer-wer-wer...*an ostrich with chestnut stripes and a tree growing out of its head*!'

Everyone stopped and glared at him.

'Trust you to come up with something really *silly*,' said Serise, in disgust.

Jack's eyes bulged with the unfairness of that.

'Well, it's not *my* fault, is it?' he demanded. 'It's not my fault I've been put under a spell by a *large fluffy rabbit with free wifi reception*! Oh, blow it! I mean by a *gold-plated washing machine with hiccups*—I mean—I mean—by a you-know-what! Is it?'

'Well, at least the rest of us aren't being stupid about it,' said Anil. 'At least we're just saying words like *watch* or *wish*, or *daffodil singing the National Anthem with a straw up its nostril*.'

He stopped and looked a bit baffled.

'But what are we going to do?' asked Winsome, alarmed. 'Miss Broom has cast a spell on us, and that means we can't even tell anyone.'

Rodney Wright scratched his head.

'You're all nuts,' he said. 'Totally bonkers.'

Anil suddenly began to look hopeful.

'Can *you* say it, Rodney?' he asked.

'Yes!' exclaimed Winsome. 'Perhaps Rodney escaped the spell because he was trapped in the cupboard.'

'Say it,' said Jack. 'Go on! Go on, Rodney! Say it!'

Rodney sighed. 'Say what?'

'That Miss Broom is a…is a…you know.'

'Miss Broom is a you know?'

'Perhaps we could write it down,' said Winsome.

But even when Slacker had found an old doughnut bag in his pocket, and someone else had gone and swiped a biro from the dinner ladies' register, all Winsome found she could write was

## MISS BROOM IS A WIT

—and then the biro stopped working.

'Tut!' said Anil. 'Give that pen here!'

His effort spelled out:

## MISS BROOM IS A TWIT

Which was quite pleasing, but not a lot of help.

'Perhaps we could find some way of letting people know without saying the words,' suggested Emily.

Winsome considered. 'You mean, like a mime or something?'

'Oh yes,' said Serise, very sarcastic. 'We'll probably all end up acting like mad bluebottles. Anyway, who could we tell?'

They all looked at each other, and there was silence apart from the sound of Rodney scratching at his head again.

'Mrs Elwig?' suggested Slacker. Mrs Elwig was the headteacher.

Anil rolled his eyes. 'Slacker, Mrs Elwig is always looking in a mirror and combing her long golden hair,' he said. 'She travels about in a wheelchair with a blanket over her, so no-one has ever seen her legs, and she smells of fish. She's hardly going to start objecting to the fact that one of her teachers is a *stitch*, is she? Even if we could get the words out.'

'Well, at least we know why last year's Class Six never told anyone about Miss Broom,' said Winsome sadly.

Everyone nodded.

'Hey,' said Jack. 'Do you remember when last year's Class Six put on that production of *The Wizard of Oz* in the playground where the wicked wer-wer-wer—oh blast it!—the thingammyjigs of the east and west were actually gibbons? Because I always thought that was a bit odd.'

Winsome sighed.

'We'll just have to hope for the best,' she said. 'And after all, we *are* all whizzes at maths now.'

'Hey, Rodney!' said Jack. 'What's fifty-six times eighteen?'

*A thousand and eight*, everyone in Class Six except Rodney murmured, still slightly wonderingly.

Rodney was too busy scratching his head to reply.

# CHAPTER SIX

When Class Six got back to class at the end of lunch they sat down in their places, folded their arms, sat up straight, and tried to look as uninteresting as traffic cones.

Luckily they were all wearing bright orange sweatshirts, which helped.

At least, they all tried to look like traffic cones apart from Rodney. Rodney shambled in after all the others, still scratching his head.

'Hurry up and sit down!' said Emily anxiously. 'Miss Broom will be here soon!'

Rodney nodded, and immediately tripped over the edge of the carpet.

'Watch out!' everybody hissed, as he clutched at

Miss Broom's desk to stop himself falling over. 'You don't want to upset Algernon!'

Rodney steadied himself. It was strange, but his eyes looked a bit red. No. They actually looked a bit *purple*.

'I think I might be going to be ill,' he said, a bit puzzled. 'Everything keeps turning round like windmills, and it's making me feel sick.'

Winsome got up and led Rodney to his place.

'You sit quietly,' she said. 'It's probably just the shock of having a school dinner after all those weeks of home cooking.'

Slacker grunted.

'You don't get enough in a school dinner to make anyone feel anything,' he said. 'Except hungry.'

Serise leant away from Rodney as he went past her.

'I hope he hasn't gone and caught anything in that cupboard,' she said.

Rodney sat down rather suddenly when he got to his place.

'I feel sort of...' he said. **'I feel sort of—'**

Everyone jumped. Rodney's voice had suddenly gone very deep and loud. Instead of sounding like a puzzled duck, as usual, he sounded like a cow mooing up from the bottom of a well.

Even Rodney noticed something was different.

**'That's funny,'** he said, his voice booming out like a foghorn.

Class Six nearly hit the roof.

'Shhh!' they hissed, frantically. 'Don't make so much noise!'

Rodney frowned.

**'But—'** he began.

His voice was getting louder with every word he spoke.

'If he goes on like that he'll end up cracking the ceiling and bringing the roof down on us!' said Anil.

Emily whimpered. Serise turned round and leant over Rodney's desk.

'Keep *quiet*,' she hissed fiercely. 'Because if you say one single word from now on I'll bash you over the head with my library book. Do you understand?'

Rodney took in a breath, but everyone said *shhhh!* again and he closed his mouth. He was stupid in lots of ways, but his memory was all right, and Serise had hit him over the head with her library book before.

'But he can't just not say anything at all! He *can't*!' said Emily, in a panic. 'What if Miss Broom asks him a question?'

'That won't matter,' said Anil. 'He can never answer questions anyway.'

'But he's going to have to answer the register,' said Winsome. 'What can we *do*?'

Class Six looked at each other, but the only sound in the whole classroom was Rodney's nails scratching at his scalp.

Anil frowned. 'You know, I think Serise is right. Rodney *must* have caught something when he was in the cupboard. Perhaps a spider bit him, or he breathed in some poison dust, or some cauldron gloop got on his fingers and he didn't wash his hands before lunch.'

Serise scowled at Rodney.

'*Did* you wash your hands before lunch?' she demanded.

Rodney opened his mouth, remembered about the library book, and shook his head.

'So what can we do?' asked Jack. 'What can we do? Miss Broom will be here any minute, and *what can we do*?'

'You'll have to answer for him,' said Anil.

'Me?' asked Jack, appalled.

'Yes. You sit next to him. Whenever Miss Broom asks Rodney a question, you'll have to sort of lean over and say the answer.'

'But she'll see my lips moving,' objected Jack. 'All I can say without my lips moving is *gottle o' geer*!'

'Well then, everyone in front of Rodney and Jack will have to sway sideways so Miss Broom can't see their lips. OK? But try to do it naturally, so Miss Broom doesn't notice anything odd.'

Everyone looked at each other. None of them looked happy.

'Or,' said Anil, 'if anyone's got a better idea...'

But no-one had.

★ ★ ★

The afternoon was torture.

'Rodney?' asked Miss Broom. 'What's your middle name, please, dear? I can't quite read what it says in the register.'

Class Six swayed gently towards the middle of the room and Anil dug Jack in the ribs.

'Er...horsemeat!' blurted out Jack, mad with fright.

Jack wasn't as stupid as Rodney, but sometimes he got close.

Miss Broom frowned and peered at the register.

'Really?' she said. 'I think I must need some new glasses. It looks more like *Cedric* to me.'

'Rodney?' asked Miss Broom, a bit later, when Class Six were learning about Healthy Eating. 'What's *your* favourite sort of fruit, dear?'

Class Six relaxed a little. That was a question anyone could answer. Jack only had to say *apple*, like nearly everybody else.

'Er...conkers!' said Jack, white with panic.

Luckily Miss Broom laughed, but Class Six nearly exploded from sheer tension.

'Rodney, dear!' Miss Broom asked soon afterwards. 'What do *you* eat for breakfast?'

Class Six crossed their fingers as they swayed gently across in front of Rodney and Jack.

'Florn cakes!' said Jack, his tongue in a tangle of terror.

Serise rolled her eyes as Miss Broom looked at Rodney in surprise.

'*Florn* cakes?' she echoed. 'How interesting. And delicious. But you know, *I* thought the only way to get to Florn was on a broomstick.'

★ ★ ★

'Phew!' said Winsome, when Class Six finally tottered out into the playground. 'Home time. We made it!'

Emily was white and shaking.

'All those monkeys were really scary,' she said.

'Nice bananas, though,' said Slacker with satisfaction.

'But what are we going to do about Rodney?' demanded Serise. 'Jack can't keep answering for Rodney for a whole school year. He was rubbish enough at it for one afternoon.'

Winsome sighed. 'You're right,' she said. 'Miss Broom will notice before long.'

Everyone looked at Rodney, who was shambling along looking clumsy and confused. Well, at least that was normal.

Anil put his head on one side.

'I don't think he's looking quite such an odd colour,' he said. 'He went really bright plum purple when we were having story time, but he's a softer sort of shade, now. More like a mouldy potato.'

'Perhaps he's getting better,' said Winsome, hopefully. 'Rodney, try not to talk to anyone, all right? When your mum asks you if you've had a good day at school, just grunt a bit. And then by tomorrow you might be feeling better.'

Rodney nodded, scratching his head.

'And that's all we can do, is it?' asked Serise scornfully. 'Hope he gets better?'

Winsome shrugged. 'Well, people do usually get better from most things,' she pointed out. 'Whatever Rodney's caught, it'll probably wear off.'

Serise snorted.

'What Rodney's got is a dose of magic,' she said. 'And I doubt very much that a good night's sleep is going to have much effect on that!'

And she turned and walked off.

# CHAPTER SEVEN

'So,' said Winsome's mum, when she got home from work. 'How was your first day in Class Six, Winsome?'

Winsome thought about it.

'Exciting,' she said.

'Well, education *is* exciting. What did you study?'

'Oh, quite a lot of things,' said Winsome. 'Times tables, to start with. I can even do sums like fifteen times twenty-nine now. In my head.'

Winsome's mum beamed proudly. 'Wonderful! If you carry on like that you'll get right to the top, girl, just where you should be.'

The top of what? Winsome wondered. She'd always hoped she might get to be a doctor, but now it looked as if she might end up being something quite different. Like a rat. Or a toadstool.

'And Miss Broom?' went on Mrs Lee. 'How is she?'

Winsome opened her mouth to tell her. But then she only said, 'She's pretty exciting, too.'

★ ★ ★

Slacker Punchkin's family didn't really talk to each other much. Their mouths were usually too full. But Slacker's very big sister Violet did stop chewing for a moment to ask, 'How was Miss Broom?'

Slacker shifted his vast shoulders in a shrug. There was no need to say anything. Violet was two years older than he was: she must know all about Miss Broom. So why oh why oh why hadn't she *told* him?

Ah yes. Of course.

'A bit pointy-hatted,' he mumbled, through a cream cake.

Violet nodded with perfect understanding. 'Algernon still around?' she asked.

He nodded back, glumly.

'Hmm,' said Violet. 'Well, you'll probably be all right. Just so long as you're careful. As long as you're *very* careful.'

Slacker reached out for another cream cake. He needed to keep his strength up, and his wits about him, too.

He was going to be very very *very* careful.

★ ★ ★

Serise's little brother and sister wanted to hear all about her first day with Miss Broom.

Serise thought about telling them about it—but the last thing she wanted was Floriss and Morris waking up screaming in the middle of the night, so she just told them Miss Broom was a bit like a godmother from a fairy tale.

'Aaah,' said Serise's mum fondly, when Serise had gone to bed. 'Serise is such a lovely little girl. So kind to her little brother and sister.'

Serise's dad hadn't noticed many signs of Serise being kind to anyone.

But he was even more scared of his wife than he was of Serise, so he didn't say anything at all.

★ ★ ★

Emily *did* wake up screaming, so she spent the rest of the night with her mum.

★ ★ ★

Rodney's mum and dad both worked late on a Monday, so he had his supper at Mrs Giddings' house. Mrs Giddings was all right, but luckily Mr Giddings hated anyone talking while the telly was on.

That was why neither of them realised that Rodney's voice had gone as deep as a giant's burp.

When Rodney took his socks off that night he discovered that his toes had turned green, too.

The worst thing, though, was that his head was still itching and itching and *itching*.

★ ★ ★

Anil spent the evening on the internet. He discovered eighty-seven different ways to get rid of witches, but some of them were impossible (where on earth could you get unicorn's horn?) and some were certainly illegal. Worse than that, some of them were extremely risky.

It took him ages to get to sleep.

★ ★ ★

Jack went to his gran's house on a Monday. She was doing her judo exercises, as usual, so he helped himself to a biscuit and watched TV.

'So, how was it?' asked Gran, when she had finished beating up invisible villains. 'Miss Broom all right, is she?'

'Awesome,' said Jack. And then stopped and listened to what he'd just said. He'd meant to say aw*ful*, but it had come out wrong.

He tried again.

'Awful,' (yes, he could say it!)

Except that somehow his voice had carried on all by itself: '—ly good,' he said.

Gran looked surprised. Jack liked lots of things—fighting Gran at judo, football, trains, and spaghetti bolognese—but she had never known him be very enthusiastic about school before.

It wasn't even as if he *looked* enthusiastic. His face had gone bright red, as if he was being strangled by an invisible snake.

'Miss Broom,' he went on, hoarsely, as if the words were tying knots round his tonsils. 'She's...a...wer...wer...*washing machine*!'

'A what?'

Jack tried again.

'She's a...a...a *witchetty-grub*! A *weeble-dooly*! A...a...a...*wurlitzer*!'

Gran looked impressed.

'Amazing, the words they teach you at school, nowadays,' she said. 'But you be careful, boy: too much knowledge can melt your brains like jelly fritters, you know.'

By that time Jack had a strong feeling as if his nose was about to explode, so he gave up, exhausted.

Jack had never been clever, but three things were clear to him. Firstly, Miss Broom *was* a witch. Secondly, as he couldn't tell anyone, he couldn't get anyone to help him.

And thirdly, unless he used what few brains he had really carefully he was going to end up in deep, deep trouble.

# CHAPTER EIGHT

The next morning Class Six gathered in the bright cold of the playground. Most of the children looked as if they hadn't got much sleep, but Anil seemed rather pleased with himself.

'I bet my brother five pounds I could do any times sum he gave me in my head within five seconds,' he said.

Jack's mouth fell open.

'Brilliant,' he breathed. 'Hey, I can't wait to try that on my dad!'

Anil shook his head.

'Nah,' he said. 'Look, no offence, Jack, right, but you're quite stupid, aren't you?'

'Yeah,' agreed Jack. 'So what?'

'So, no-one will believe you can do difficult sums in your head in a million years,' Anil said. 'You should ask for more a lot more than a fiver. Ask for twenty!'

Jack's eyes bulged.

'*Twenty pounds?*'

'Yeah. Stands to reason.'

Serise narrowed her eyes calculatingly. 'I think I might ask my mum for a horse.'

'But…you don't like horses,' said Winsome.

'Hmm, that's true,' admitted Serise. 'Perhaps a pair of over-the-knee boots, then. Or a new jacket. Or…'

Slacker ambled up munching a cake.

'My big sister told me to be careful with Miss Broom,' he said. 'So I've decided the best thing is to maintain a low profile.'

Anil looked up at the mountain that was Slacker Punchkin.

'Well, that's not going to be very easy,' he said. 'You've got a profile like Mount Everest. And that's when you're lying down.'

Winsome looked at her watch. 'Rodney's not here yet.'

Jack went to the gate and looked both ways along the road. 'There's no sign of him.'

Emily turned pale.

'Perhaps he's got worse,' she said. 'Perhaps they've taken him to hospital!'

'Perhaps he's scratched his head so much that his skin's worn through and he's got blood trickling all down his face,' said Jack.

'Ew!' said Serise.

Emily's face went even paler.

'Perhaps he's dead,' she whispered.

But Anil shook his head. 'There can't be anything much wrong with him,' he said. 'I mean, look over there at those mums. They're just talking to each other about quite boring things, aren't they? If Rodney had anything serious they'd be yacking and yacking and yacking.'

'That's true,' said Slacker Punchkin. 'Whenever anyone drops dead my gran can't wait to tell everyone about it.' Slacker put on a cracked old-lady voice: *"Have you heard Clint Gherkin's died?"* She always knows all about it even if it's someone in another country that no-one's ever heard of.'

Emily gave a long shaken sigh of relief.

'That's true,' she said. 'But then, where *is* Rodney?'

They all thought about it.

'Wherever he is, he's missing school,' said Jack, with a trace of envy.

'I bet he's gone to the doctor and got some banana medicine,' said Slacker, envious too.

And then the bell went and they all trooped in to class.

★ ★ ★

'Now all of you stand up, please, Class Six,' said Miss Broom, after she'd called the register. 'Good. Now I want everyone to touch their right ear with their left hand. No, their *right* ear, Jack. That's it. Now everyone try to touch the ceiling! Stretch! Excellent. And now let's try running on the spot. Come along! Left-right-left!'

Class Six ran until they felt woken up. Then they ran until they felt full of beans. At the front Miss

Broom was running too, her little plump legs in her brown stockings pumping up and down so fast that all you could see was a blur.

'Jolly good!' she cried. 'Faster!'

Class Six ran until they were scarlet in the face and they thought they might be going to explode. Even Slacker pounded away until the classroom windows were rattling in their frames.

'Marvellous!' said Miss Broom at last. 'All right, everybody, you can sit down again now.'

Class Six sank gratefully into their seats, so red in the face they looked like uniformed tomatoes. Though actually, Slacker looked more like a uniformed aubergine.

Miss Broom looked round at them all. Her eyes were sharp as holly prickles. 'Well, you're all obviously quite fit,' she said. 'That's good. For a moment I was afraid you might be allergic to my special...er...*teaching methods*, and that would have spoiled everything.'

Class Six did try to summon up a little weak coughing, but it only managed to sound pathetic and desperate.

Miss Broom waited for the noise to die down, and then she smiled, showing her sharp little pearly teeth.

'So now,' she said. 'I think it's time to do some spelling.'

And she took a black wand out of her desk drawer.

* ★ ★

Class Six sat up and blinked. There was a bell
sounding. But…

'Is that the fire alarm?' asked Slacker Punchkin
groggily.

'No, no,' said Miss Broom. 'That's the bell for
playtime. Off you go, all of you!'

Class Six, very puzzled, stumbled into the
playground. They squinted round. The sky was grey,
but it still seemed very bright.

'I think I must have been asleep,' mumbled Jack.

'Me too,' agreed Slacker, yawning like a
hippopotamus. 'Hey, hang on a minute! I was so
fast asleep I've gone and left my breaktime snack in
my backpack. There were three Fatso Bars and two
cheese pasties in there! What am I going to do now?'

Winsome was still blinking.

'But we can't *all* have fallen asleep,' she said.
'Not unless…'

'She's gone and enchanted us, hasn't she?' said
Serise, outraged.

'She must have done,' agreed Anil. 'There's no
way we'd all have fallen asleep otherwise. So the
question is, what's she done to us?'

Winsome frowned.

'Does anyone remember anything?' she said.
'Because I seem to remember all the books in the

reading corner diving off the shelves and then flapping round the classroom.'

'Yes, I remember that,' said Emily. 'And all the letters and pictures fell off the pages as they went, until they were as white as seagulls.'

Slacker grunted.

'Those letters,' he said. 'They tasted of vinegar toffee.'

Jack gasped. 'You mean you *ate* them?'

'Course I did,' said Slacker. 'It was better than letting them all dive up my nose, wasn't it? At least I got to taste them. They were quite rubbery, though.'

'I could taste them even though they went up my nose,' admitted Anil. 'But to me they tasted of peppermint.'

Winsome clutched at her hair. 'But this is impossible,' she said. 'It just *must* be a dream.'

'Yeah, and we all dreamed the same thing,' said Serise, rolling her eyes. 'That was no dream, Winsome. That was wa-wa-wa-*wigglecraft*.'

'I remember, now!' exclaimed Anil. 'She got a wand out of her drawer and then she said something about spells.'

'No, not spells,' said Jack. '*Spelling!*'

And then Class Six were chattering as fast as they could, remembering the taste of the spiky letters and the sound of the books flapping round the room.

Suddenly Emily gasped.

'I can spell *necessary*,' she announced in amazement.

Everyone stopped chattering and thought about it.

Jack blinked. 'Hey, when I think about how to spell *necessary* two little lizards sort of pop up in front of my eyes holding a banner with the word NECESSARY written on it.'

'Red lizards, wearing green ties?' asked Slacker.

'That's right. On pogo sticks.'

Class Six all stood and thought, and then Serise let out a small shriek.

'I can spell anything!' she said. 'Even *queue*!'

'And *meringue*,' said Slacker Punchkin, licking his lips.

Jack began jumping up and down.

'I can spell anything at all!' he shouted. 'Anything! I can even spell... I can spell... I can even spell *DIARRHOEA*!'

And then he stopped jumping about quite suddenly and looked a bit puzzled for a moment. And then he put up his hand to his head and he began to scratch and scratch and scratch.

# CHAPTER NINE

'I don't know what it is, but it itches like mad,' said Jack.

'You'll have to sit at the back of the class and hope Miss Broom doesn't notice you,' said Winsome, despairingly.

'A fat lot of good that's going to do,' muttered Serise. 'Jack's gone and caught Rodney's lurgy, that's what's happened. And if it's that catching then we'll *all* be getting it!'

Anil hunched his shoulders.

'We're going to die, then,' he said.

'Nooooo!' shrieked nearly everyone. '*I don't want to die!*'

But Winsome drew herself up bravely.

'We don't know what's going to happen,' she said. 'And don't forget that Anil's always looking on the bad side. Remember the time he said Mr Wolfe had grown a tail? And that turned out not to be true.'

'You don't know that,' said Anil. 'He probably keeps it tucked down inside his trousers.'

'Or the time Anil said that when he went to the seaside he saw Mrs Elwig swimming in the sea with a pod of killer whales? And then when we got back to school there Mrs Elwig was, as usual.'

'Sitting in her wheelchair smelling of fish,' muttered Anil. 'With a rug over her legs, singing songs about sailors, and hardly ever bothering to breathe.'

Winsome waved all that away.

'And as for Rodney,' she said, 'we'd have heard if he'd dropped dead. You know what grown ups are like, they'd have been talking about nothing else. Rodney will be—'

'Over there!' screeched Jack, pointing.

And there he was, just getting out of his mum's car.

'But...that can't be Rodney,' said Emily. 'That's someone with black hair.'

They watched Rodney walk through the school gate. When he got closer they could see that his hair wasn't really black—it had purple and green glossy streaks, like a magpie's back.

There was something else a bit odd about him, too, but it took Class Six a while to work out what it was.

'Your nose has got bigger!' said Emily, in horror. 'It's…it's…'

'It looks a bit like a trunk,' said Serise.

It was only a very small trunk, but there was no doubt about it.

'Yes,' said Rodney. 'My mum took me to the doctor's, but he says it's nothing to worry about.'

'Well, at least your voice is back to normal,' said Winsome. 'Perhaps all these other symptoms will go away by themselves too.'

Rodney shrugged.

'It is quite odd, though,' he told them. 'Because my toes have gone bright green. And when I sneeze…'

As he said it his trunk began to twitch and his face got redder and redder. Class Six all screamed, and they were throwing themselves sideways when it happened. There was a sound like someone punching a sack of flour, and Rodney sneezed.

Inwards.

His trunk shrunk until it was the size of a surprised caterpillar, and his belly ballooned outwards. There was a whole series of small explosions as the buttons on his shirt popped off.

One other thing happened, too. His ears shot out from the sides of his head as they were if on elastic

—and then they whizzed back into place again with a sharp and painful snap.

Class Six got up slowly from where they'd thrown themselves out of the way of Rodney's sneeze.

'Well, at least if Rodney's sneezes are going inwards then he isn't going to give us anything nasty,' said Winsome.

'But he already has!' squeaked Emily. 'Look at Jack. He keeps scratching and scratching, and that's what Rodney was doing yesterday.'

Jack shrugged, and scratched some more.

'I've only got an itchy head,' he said. 'It's probably a case of galloping dandruff or something. Or nits.'

Slacker shook his chins. 'That's not nits,' he said. 'Nits are ordinary, like veruccas and tooth rot. They don't make your nose get bigger.'

'They don't make your toes turn bright green, either,' said Serise.

'Ordinary nits don't,' agreed Anil. 'But don't forget Rodney was wearing Miss Broom's hat yesterday. Perhaps he caught them from that. Special wer-wer-wer—oh bother it! Special *magic* nits.'

Class Six exchanged glances.

'Jack did have his head really close to Rodney's yesterday when he was answering for him,' said Winsome. 'He could have caught them then.'

Jack scratched his head again, and as he did everyone else's scalps began itching and itching in sympathy. Class Six folded their arms and gritted their teeth and vowed that they weren't going to start scratching. This tickling was just in their minds. It was. It *was*.

'I don't want to get magic nits!' whimpered Emily. 'I don't!'

Everyone's shoulders had begun to twitch, now, as the itchiness of their scalps got worse. It felt as if little spiders were crawling through the roots of their hair. As if tiny needles were pricking into the skin. And they just had to...

'This is terrible,' said Anil, suddenly. 'If these are nits then they're incredibly powerful nits. These are NITS OF DOOM!'

And at last Class Six put their hands up to their heads and began to scratch and scratch and scratch.

# CHAPTER TEN

As soon as Miss Broom arrived in the classroom she gave out lumps of modelling clay and asked Class Six to write stories. Everyone was so keen not to attract Miss Broom's attention that they sat as still as statues, apart from the occasional twitch and wriggle to try to soothe away the itching, and wrote like mad.

Writing a story was easier than usual because the lumps of clay squeezed themselves into the shape of everything they wrote about and acted out the story for them.

Ten of Class Six's stories were about football, seven were about ponies, six were about winning talent shows, six were about bullying and one was about cake.

None of them was anything at all to do with witches or magic of any kind.

'You're *such* good children,' said Miss Broom, when the bell had gone and Class Six still carried on writing even though their clay figures had rolled themselves back into balls and thrown themselves neatly into the clay bin. 'But it's time for lunch now.'

By that time Jack's nose was beginning to wobble slightly whenever he turned his head and Rodney's was so long it kept getting in the way when he was trying to eat his pizza.

Class Six edged their chairs as far away from Rodney and Jack as they could, but everyone's scalps were still itching and it was ever so hard not to scratch all the time.

'What's it like, having a trunk?' asked Anil.

'All right,' said Rodney. 'Except I can tell that this pizza smells of mice and drains.'

**'And burning,'** said Jack—and then clapped his hand to his mouth because his voice had come out in a great huge burp that echoed round like a moose in a drainpipe.

'Who's making that row?' snapped Mrs Barnett from the hatch, crossly brandishing her ladle. 'Stop it at once or I'll send for Mrs Elwig!'

Serise went to scratch her head, and then didn't. The whole class kept bringing their hands up towards their heads and then pretending they just wanted to wave at someone. All the little kids in Class Three kept half-waving back and then looking behind them. They were getting really confused.

Anil put down his knife and fork.

'This is terrible,' he said. 'There's no getting away from it. We all must have caught it.'

Emily began to cry.

'I don't want a trunk!' she wailed. 'I don't want a big burpy voice. I like my toes the colour they are!'

Winsome gave her a hug.

be all right,' she said bravely. 'Rodney's voice
ck to normal, so that shows he's getting better.'
'But look at his nose!' said Serise. 'I bet he can
sniff the crumbs off his own chin.'

Rodney looked pleased, and tried it.

'I can, as well,' he said proudly. But the crumbs
must have irritated the inside of his nose, because it
began to wobble and twitch.

'He's going to sneeze!' shouted Jack. 'Watch out,
he's going to sneeze!'

Everyone tried to get out of the way, but the
dining room chairs were so squeezed together that
there wasn't room. Jack tried to duck and ended
up dunking the end of his nose in his custard, and
Winsome tore off a button when she tried to get
under the table.

Slacker and Serise, both wedged in helplessly, each
got bashed on the side of the head by one of Rodney's
elastic ears.

★ ★ ★

Class Six stood in the playground, keeping plenty
of distance between them, with their arms folded to
stop themselves scratching their heads. The rest of
the school were playing happily in the sun, but Class
Six didn't feel like playing at all.

'But what can we *do?*' asked Emily, in despair.

'If we told our mums they'd get us some nit cream,' suggested Jack.

Anil shook his head.

'That'd kill ordinary nits,' he said. 'But these... these are different. I mean, they've turned Rodney's toes green, so they must have got deep down into his system. Nit cream won't help with that.'

Slacker Punchkin heaved a sigh.

'How can you stop magic?' he asked.

'Horseshoes are supposed to work,' said Emily.

'Oh, that's all right, then,' said Anil. 'In that case all we have to do is look out for a horse next time we're at the shops and persuade it to let us borrow some of its footwear.'

Winsome frowned thoughtfully. 'I think I've read somewhere that woo-woo-woo—magic people hate rowan twigs.'

'Who?' asked Slacker.

'Not who, *what*,' Winsome explained. 'A rowan's a sort of tree. It has bunches of red berries on in the autumn. And wik-wik—oh, bother—*wickets* are supposed to hate it.'

Jack's nose twitched. 'I think my granddad's got one in his garden,' he said.

'Really?' asked Emily, quite hopeful. 'Where does he live?'

'Canada,' said Jack.

Everyone stopped looking hopeful.

'But aren't there any rowan trees near here?' asked Serise.

Anil rolled his eyes. 'Of course not. We wouldn't have a wer-wer-wer-*wiggle* in the school if there was, would we?'

Emily looked as if she was going to start crying again.

'No, it's all right,' said Winsome, hastily. She went over to the rubbish bin and pulled something out.

'Errgh!' said Serise. 'That's disgusting! Someone's drunk out of that water bottle. Eergh!'

'What's it for?' asked Slacker, scratching his head.

'It's to make into a wer-wer-wer-*widget* bottle,' said Winsome, mysteriously.

'A what?'

'A wer-wer-wer, a wer-wer-wer, a—oh, blow it! A cauldron-owner's bottle. To keep cauldron-owners away,' said Winsome. 'And if it keeps *them* away then it'll probably wipe out other sorts of magic, too.'

'A plastic water bottle?' said Anil, doubtfully.

'Well, we have to fill it up, first,' said Winsome.

And she led the way to the long jump pit.

★ ★ ★

A witch bottle had to be filled with sand, which was easy, and rosemary, which was easy too. It grew in the wildlife garden because it was good for the bees.

'What else do we need?' asked Jack.

'Pins,' said Winsome.

'Hm,' said everybody. But then Anil said *how about drawing pins?* and then it was just a matter of getting Slacker Punchkin to stand in front of the notice board on the way back along the corridor to class so that Jack, who was skinny and little, could borrow a few without anyone noticing.

'So what do we do now?' asked Serise, when Anil had poked the drawing pins down into the sand-and-rosemary mixture inside the bottle and screwed the top back on. Miss Broom hadn't arrived in class yet.

'Put it up the chimney,' said Winsome. 'That's what it said in the wer-wer-wer-*winkle* book I read once.'

Everyone looked round hurriedly. The classroom was mostly windows, and the bits that weren't windows were cupboards or display boards.

'Well, inside a wall will do,' said Winsome.

Slacker Punchkin thumped on the wall beside him with a vast meaty fist.

'I think I could punch a hole through this,' he said. 'We could take down this poster of a werewolf and then stick it up again once we've hidden the wer-wer-wer-*welly* bottle.'

'Idiot,' snapped Serise. 'Knocking a hole in that wall will take you straight through to Mr Bloodsworth's class. And *he's* a vampire.'

Class Six had never been taught by Mr Bloodsworth, but there had been rumours about him ever since he'd arrived last year.

'Don't do it,' Jack advised Slacker. 'I mean, just think about the amount of blood you've got in you. I bet you look like a walking feast to Mr Bloodsworth. Like a big pile of doughnuts.'

'Slacker looks like a big pile of doughnuts to everyone,' muttered Serise.

'Quick!' said Emily, as footsteps sounded in the corridor. 'She's coming! *Quick!*'

Anil hastily shoved the witch bottle into a drawer and then joined everyone in rushing to sit down and fold their arms.

'That was really brave putting the wer-wer-wer-*wolf* bottle in your drawer,' whispered Winsome to Anil, as Miss Broom's bosom appeared in the doorway. 'If Miss Broom finds it she might cast a spell on you!'

Anil looked at Winsome as if she was mad.

'I didn't put the bottle in *my* drawer,' he told her. 'Do you think I'm nuts? I put it in Rodney's.'

'*What*?' said Winsome.

'Well, he's under a spell anyway. And he doesn't even believe in wer-wer-wer-*wigwams*, does he?'

# CHAPTER ELEVEN

Class Six sat, agog to see what effect the magic bottle would have.

Miss Broom went and sat at her desk. She opened the register.

And then she twitched.

She looked round searchingly. Class Six did their traffic cone impersonations.

'That's very odd,' Miss Broom said. 'I've got ever such a funny feeling as if...'

She sniffed the air.

'... as if someone's put me in a plastic bubble,' she went on. 'As if I can't breathe properly.'

Her desk drawer slid itself open and Algernon's head appeared. He slid smoothly up her arm and draped himself round her neck like a fat scarf.

Miss Broom stroked Algernon thoughtfully.

'What?' she said. 'They've done what? Really? Where? Great mushrooms of Basingstoke! No wonder, then. Would you mind, Algernon, dear?'

Algernon rippled down Miss Broom's other arm and powerfully across her desk towards Class Six.

'Do keep quite still, dears,' said Miss Broom, kindly. 'We don't want Algernon to bite you.'

Algernon was on Winsome's desk, now. Winsome kept as still as a frozen fish finger as he crawled up her arm and across her shoulders. Then Algernon crawled down her other arm and onto Emily's desk.

Emily was a real cry-baby. She was frightened of everything, even paper clips. Emily was going to panic and scream and then Algernon would bite her with his sharp bright fangs, and...

Emily gulped in a huge deep breath, opened her mouth wide—and then closed it again. Class Six could actually see the screams bulging about inside her tummy, but none of them came out. Not one. Not even when Algernon slid up her front and gazed into her eyes before aiming under her left ear and onwards towards the other side of the classroom.

Algernon made his way straight over the desks to Rodney's drawer and slid into it through the cut-out handle. He was too big to do that, but he did it anyway. The next thing Class Six knew, Algernon was coming out again with the witch bottle held between his jaws.

Then, almost too quickly to see, Algernon threw the bottle into the air, and as it came down again the snake's head struck out so fast that all Class Six saw was a blur of orange. And then the bottle was on the floor in pieces, and all the sand and rosemary and drawing pins were scattered all over the carpet.

Miss Broom heaved a huge sigh.

'Thank you, Algernon,' she said. 'Oh dear, though, what a dreadful thing to find in the classroom. I wonder how it got here.'

Her orange eyes swept round the class. Everyone tried their hardest to shrink down behind their desks. It was much harder for Slacker than any of the others, but Slacker wasn't where Miss Broom's eyes stopped.

They stopped on Anil, whose teeth started to chatter like icicles in an earthquake.

Miss Broom looked at Anil very carefully, and as she did, Anil began to change. First of all Class Six found they could see the veins under his skin wriggling through his muscles; and then they found they could see his bones; and then they could see all his insides. His heart was pumping away like anything. Class Six could even see the mixture of

pizza and custard that was being squeezed gently backwards and forwards in his stomach.

Everyone opened their mouths to say *eeergh*—and then didn't dare.

Now Anil's skull had changed to something like ripply glass, and inside there was a grey thing like a giant curled-up prawn. There were lots of tiny bits of forked lightning flicking through it, and just sometimes, like a cloud, you could see the shape of a football, or a laptop, or a stuffed rabbit.

And then Miss Broom gave a sharp I-thought-so sniff and Anil was back to normal, except for being a bit pale and cross-eyed.

'I see,' said Miss Broom. 'This is very clever of you, my dears, but really, you mustn't worry. Why, you should be delighted and overjoyed. Just think, you've got a teacher who's a witch. That's wonderful. Magical. Remember all those boring lessons where you've sat there trying to learn the capital of Outer Mongolia, or when Richard the Third died, or how to use capital letters? Why, with a small spell, I can make it so you never make a mistake with capital letters again. I can make it so you never forget about Ulan Bator, or what happened in 1485. Yes, being a witch is the best thing ever. Being a witch means I can do anything at all! Anything I like!'

Class Six sank as far as they could get behind their desks.

Miss Broom could do anything she liked?

Yes. That was what they were all afraid of.

* * *

'What have you stuck on your face?' demanded Rodney's gran irritably that evening. 'You look like something from outer space!'

Rodney looked at himself in the mirror. He had antennae with scarlet pom-poms on the ends growing out of his forehead. Gran was right. He *did* look like something from outer space.

'That's funny,' he said. 'I can't remember ever going in a space ship. I suppose it must have been ages ago, when I was too young to remember.'

'And stop making your eyes spin round in circles!' snapped Gran. 'It's enough to put me off my tea.'

'Is it?' asked Rodney, brightening. 'So can I eat your piece of cake, then?'

'Don't be daft,' said Gran.

# CHAPTER TWELVE

'My mum put gunky stuff all over my head last night to get rid of the nits,' Jack reported glumly in the playground the next morning. 'It stank like anything. And *then* my mum didn't find any nits in the comb afterwards, so it was all a waste of time.'

'These nits are bound to be immune to ordinary nit-gunk,' said Winsome.

'They're probably immune to everything,' said Anil, who was looking as if he hadn't slept much.

'Yes,' sighed Jack. 'It'd probably take a nuclear explosion to wipe out these wer-wer-wer—oh blast it, these *whatever* nits.'

Serise was giving Anil a suspicious look.

'Your voice is beginning to sound a bit deep,' she said. 'You haven't caught it too, have you?'

'No I *haven't!*' snapped Anil—but his voice boomed on the last word like an owl in an oil drum and made everyone jump.

'Oh all right, all right,' he went on, crossly. 'Last night I sounded as if I'd got a man-sized frog in my throat, but I haven't got nits, any more than Jack has. I combed through my hair three times over a sheet of paper and not one single nit fell out.'

'Well, whatever it is, you can keep away from me,' said Serise. 'I don't want them, thank you very much.'

Emily looked round anxiously.

'Where's Rodney?' she asked. 'Do you think his mum's taken him back to the doctor's?'

'No, it's all right,' said Slacker Punchkin. 'He's gone to check himself out in the loos.'

'Why?' asked Anil, sharply. 'What's happened to him now?'

Slacker shrugged. 'Nothing really bad.'

**'What's happened to him?'** asked Anil again, his voice booming round the playground like an anguished tuba.

'Well, apparently he grew antennae last night, but they've mostly gone, now. The thing is...'

'He's coming out!' gasped Winsome.

And, sure enough, there was Rodney coming out of the school building.

At least, it was someone wearing Rodney's coat. And carrying Rodney's bag. But...

Serise gulped.

'No,' she muttered. 'Not that. Please. Anything. *Anything* but that!'

Beside him, Anil went the colour of vanilla fudge.

Because Rodney had come out in huge brown spots.

Rodney slunk across the playground in long powerful strides. When he got closer the others could see that his face had gone all velvety and golden.

'Are you growing hair all over?' asked Jack.

'Well, you do as you get older,' said Rodney.

'Men are hairy,' pointed out Anil. 'They aren't furry with big brown spots.'

Rodney shrugged. 'I suppose I must be special, then.'

Miss Broom didn't seem to notice that the person who answered to Rodney's name in the register had a developed an all-over coat of shining velvet fur.

That wasn't all that had changed about Rodney, either. It was difficult to pin down exactly what else was different, but suddenly Rodney was almost...graceful.

At least his trunk had shrunk overnight until all that was left was a thing like a peach-flavour wine gum, so that was something. 'I expect he'll be back to normal soon,' said Anil, as bravely as he could.

He was speaking in a whisper that fooled no-one. 'I mean, his *voice* went back, didn't it. By tomorrow he'll probably be completely all right.'

'Unless he's dead,' put in Serise, spitefully.

And then she reached up and scratched her head hard.

★  ★  ★

Class Six had PE that morning. They trudged grimly into the hall—all except for Rodney, who showed a surprising tendency to pounce on people's shoe laces. But Miss Broom was so busy unwinding the ropes and pulling out the vaulting horse that she didn't notice.

Miss Broom dusted off her hands and turned to the class.

'Now, Class Six,' she said, 'I think we'll start with a short warm-up. All of you place yourselves so you can't touch the person next to you.'

Class Six were as spread out as they could be anyway, but they shuffled quietly sideways, trying not to meet Miss Broom's eyes. They were reflecting swooping pterodactyls at that moment, though, and it was hard to look away.

'Good. Now, I want you all to copy me. Ready? *One! Two! A one two three!*'

Class Six did their best to follow Miss Broom. To start with she held up one hand up like a policeman trying to stop traffic, and then she wound her other hand round in the air like someone twirling a sparkler.

Three little stamps with the left foot, then hop onto the right. Repeat twice. Waddle forward seven steps with the toes turned outwards, point your elbows forward as far as you could, twitch your mouth right–left–right–centre and then left again.

Hop up and down on the left foot while chanting after Miss Broom:

*'Hocus-pocus*
*Custard pie*
*A bird can fly*
*And so can—**EEEEK!**'*

The last bit wasn't anything to do with Miss Broom. The last bit was the screech everyone made when the floor got suddenly lighter under their feet and they found themselves shooting upwards, away from the polished parquet tiles.

Class Six came to a stop about half a metre up, and all you could hear after the echo of the scream had died away was the soft thudding of people's gym shoes falling down to the floor.

'That's right, dears,' said Miss Broom, smiling round at them. 'Do kick your shoes off. We don't want them falling down and hurting anyone, do we?'

Class Six stared at each other. They all had pale faces and a hanging-from-a-coathanger look. Everyone's hair, affected by Miss Broom's spell, was standing on end, so that they looked like toilet brushes.

Miss Broom looked round with great satisfaction.

'Excellent,' she said. 'Now. Right arm up in the air, everyone and then, *scoop* downwards. That's it. Now the other arm. Good. Good. Watch where you're going, Slacker, dear!'

And Class Six were having their first ever flying lesson.

It was scary for about twenty seconds, until they worked out how to stop themselves rolling giddily round and round. And then they got the hang of scooping themselves along, and suddenly they were having the most fun they'd ever had, including that time in Year Two when Mr Holiday spilled glue all down his trousers.

The whole room was filled with great big grins, and children swooping through the air going *wheeeeee!*

Miss Broom sat herself down on a window sill and began to drink a cup of tea that had appeared from somewhere or other, and Class Six did every flying experiment they could think of. What they *couldn't* do was land—when you got to within about half a metre of the floor the air went all thick, like sponge cake, and you sort of bounced back off it. It was the same with the ceiling and the walls. All in all, it was like being on a huge bouncy castle where you never came down to earth.

Only better. Much, much better.

Emily found she could use one of the curtain rods as a barre for aerial ballet, and some of the boys discovered that they could use the vaulting horse to do the sort of somersaults and spins that would have won them Olympic gold medals in no time flat. Winsome flew determined, fast circuits of the room,

and Slacker lay back on the air and managed to find a way to rock himself gently from side to side just as if he were in a hammock.

Serise and some of the other girls raced each other in slaloms through the gym ropes, moving as easily as a shoal of fish.

It was brilliant. It was tremendous. It was wonderful. It was out of this…

Miss Broom stood up, threw her cup and saucer over her shoulder, where it vanished, and beamed round at them all.

'Standing up straight, now, all of you,' she said. 'I'm afraid it's time to go back to class.'

At once everyone in Class Six felt an odd feeling in their insides as if something had been punctured. And they began to sink. Down and down and down…

The floor felt very hard under their feet.

'Now, find your gym shoes, please,' said Miss Broom. 'We've got to go across the playground.'

The children's arms and legs felt heavy. Pulling on their gym shoes was really hard work.

'Yes, flying is very tiring, at first,' said Miss Broom, as if she had read their minds. 'You've been using muscles that have never been used in that way before. But you'll soon get used to it. Now, line up, all of you!'

Rodney ended up next to Winsome.

'Do you still believe there's no such thing as wer-wer-wer?' she asked him, grinning like a watermelon. 'As a...you know! As a pointy-hatted magic lady?'

Rodney looked surprised to be asked.

'Of course there isn't.' He frowned so his forehead wrinkled into channels of golden velvet skin, and his green eyes glowed. His teeth were looking pretty pointy, too. 'Everybody knows that.'

Winsome was used to Rodney, of course. But this time she was so astonished that she could only stand and watch him as he prowled back to class.

★ ★ ★

Just about everyone in Class Six was scratching, now. They'd given up trying to hide it. And when they answered *Good afterNOON Miss BrOOM* at afternoon registration, there was a definite hollowness to their voices which they were sure Miss Broom must notice. But she didn't.

'Are you getting a sore throat, darling?' asked Emily's mum, at home time.

'No,' said Emily. 'I think I've caught a special sort of really terrible nit.'

Emily's mum laughed.

'Sounds like me when I married your dad,' she said.

★ ★ ★

'But it can't really be nits, Slacker,' said Mrs Punchkin. 'Nits don't make your voice sound throaty.'

Slacker made a great effort. 'They do if you've caught them from a wer-wer-wer-*wombat*.'

'You could well be right, love,' agreed Mrs Punchkin. 'But I don't think we've got any wombats round here at the moment, luckily.'

Slacker clenched his great fists and tried again.

**'Miss Broom's a wreck!'** he said, all in a rush.

'I'm not surprised, having to teach you all day,' said Mrs Punchkin.

# CHAPTER THIRTEEN

Class Six ran all the way to school the next morning, and it was only partly because they wanted to find out what had happened to Rodney now.

'Can't wait to get here,' said the mothers to each other, marvelling. 'Never seen anything like it.'

'That Miss Broom must be a wonderful teacher,' said half of them.

'Yes,' replied the other half, very impressed. 'Although, tell me. What exactly *is* a woggle?'

Jack charged into the playground shouting, 'I'm growing antennae!'

'Cool!' said Anil. His voice was getting back to normal, so now he just sounded like his dad. 'Can you pick up Radio Gaga?'

'It's better than that,' said Jack. 'I can pick up League Live Match Updates!'

'Woooh!' Anil was deeply impressed. 'I can't wait for *my* antennae to grow.'

Winsome came running up. **'What are those?'** she asked, pointing at Jack's antennae, in a voice like slow gravy.

'They're digital!' boasted Jack. 'I can get about a hundred different stations, just by pushing my teeth in. It's brilliant!'

Winsome stared, between fascination and envy.

'Well, I suppose it'll be all right as long as I wear my hair in an afro,' she said musingly.

Emily came trotting across the playground to meet them. 'Hello,' she whispered.

'Has your voice gone bellowy?'

Emily nodded. 'My mum was going to take me to the doctor, but she couldn't get an appointment. The receptionist said there's a lot of it about.'

Serise flounced crossly through the school gate.

'This is just *so* annoying,' she said, as she reached them. 'I wanted to wear my silver sandals today but my toes are such a bright green I had to wear these clumpy old things instead. Look at them! I mean, they are just *so* last year!'

'Never mind,' said Winsome, comfortingly. 'The green only lasts a few hours. I was lucky, it happened overnight to me and it meant I could read in bed by the light of my own toes. I've never been able to do that before.'

Slacker ambled vastly over to them, munching. His hair was sticking up oddly above his forehead.

'Your antennae are growing, are they?' asked Jack.

Slacker smiled, displaying a large wodge of mushed crisp.

'I can get The Foodie Channel,' he said happily. 'It's fantastic. I mean, cooking—it's so *easy*. Anyone could do it. Even *I* could do it. I'm going to make a fudge sundae when I get home tonight. Topped with butterscotch popcorn and pecan brittle. And before that a carrot and peach salad with rocket, drizzled with walnut oil and decorated with nasturtium flowers. Can't wait!'

He broke off and frowned.

'Which is a bit odd, really,' he went on, thoughtfully. 'Because I don't usually go in for fruit and stuff. Hey, where's Rodney? Is he all right?'

'Oh, yeah,' said Anil carelessly. 'He just jumped up that oak tree, trying to catch a squirrel.'

When Miss Broom entered the classroom that morning she found herself greeted by thirty very excited children.

**'Good MORning Miss BrOOM,'** everyone chanted, not even bothering that they were making enough noise for a Cup Final.

'What are we going to learn today, Miss Broom?'

asked Anil. 'Because I've always wanted to know about quadratic equations.'

'No,' said Jack. 'Can't we have PE again, please, Miss?'

'Yes!' said everyone. 'PE! PE is just brilliant!'

Miss Broom looked round at them and beamed. Her orange eyes were reflecting something jumbly which might have been a bed of flowers, though it was probably a rubbish tip.

Actually, those shapes swooping backwards and forwards looked a lot like vultures. Yes. Definitely a rubbish tip.

'I'm very glad you enjoyed PE, dears,' said Miss Broom, 'but we mustn't forget the National Curriculum, must we.'

Class Six groaned.

'And that means,' said Miss Broom, 'that we need to do some Science.'

There was a moment's silence. *Science*. Well, even ordinary science could be quite interesting if it involved making bridges, or counting cars.

And as for Miss Broom's sort of science…

'What are we going to do, Miss Broom?' asked Slacker. 'Because I've always wondered how the bubbles get inside doughnuts.'

The vultures in Miss Broom's eyes did loop-the-loops. 'Well, I thought we'd do some work on habitats.'

Class Six's hearts sank.

'We did habitats in Year One, Miss Broom,' said Anil.

'And in Year Two, Miss,' said Winsome.

'And in Year Three, Four and Five,' Serise pointed out.

Miss Broom looked at them fondly. 'But have you done cockroaches?'

Emily shuddered.

'Cockroaches?' she whispered. 'But they're huge and black and they've got lots of legs. They're really *scary*.'

'And they're filthy, too,' muttered Serise. 'I'm not touching one of them. I might catch something.'

'Ah,' said Miss Broom happily, 'but my cockroaches aren't like that. They're rather out of the ordinary.'

She went to the big cupboard where Rodney had hidden and opened the door. Class Six looked, and gasped. Instead of a cauldron and a black hat, the cupboard was filled with quite ordinary shelves stacked with piles of paper and spare pens.

Miss Broom heard the gasp and turned round.

'Anything the matter, dears?' she asked.

Everybody shook their heads, and those with trunks shook those, too.

'Excellent.'

Miss Broom got down a small cardboard box, which was standing on a shelf between some exercise books and a bottle of purple ink, and took it to her desk. She folded down the front of the box, and Class Six found themselves looking into a tiny theatre. There were red velvet curtains, and even some models of small people on the stage.

And then Class Six heard something. It was quite soft to start with, and quite tinny. But it sounded...well, it *sounded* like Sahara Ice Squirrel's latest single.

Class Six craned forward to look. Those small figures—they weren't models after all. They were big black beetles. Four of them. Two were holding guitars, one was sitting at a drum kit, and the other one seemed to be the vocalist.

They were really playing Sahara Ice Squirrel, too. It was hard to see their tiny little legs moving about the fretboards of the guitars, but that drummer was certainly holding a drumstick in each of its four hands.

*Boom*, went the drum kit. *Boom. Boom snitch tara-diddle, boom snitch tara-diddle boom snitch...*

*Drrang drrang drrang dodie drrang diddle POW* went the bass guitar.

*Trrang ti todie todie trrang ti todie todie* went the lead guitar.

Class Six found themselves beginning to sway in time to the music. And then they began clicking their fingers and tapping their feet. They couldn't help it.

It was as if the music had tied strings to their arms and legs, and they just couldn't keep still.

Serise was the first one to start hand-jiving. Anil gawped at her—where'd she learned to do that?—and then, even more amazingly, Slacker suddenly jumped out of his seat, shouted '*Yeah!*' and threw himself along the aisle between the tables in a long, cool slide.

The tiny beetle band was getting louder, and as it got louder it got more and more irresistible. Anil's feet were twitching. At first he thought it was just because under his grey school socks his toes were as green as grasshoppers, but it was more than that. His toes wanted to move. To jump up and down.

His fingers had caught the itch of the music, too. They were bouncing about on his desk. Anil watched them, amazed and appalled. He had never danced in his life. He saw other people dancing sometimes, but he never joined in. He didn't know *how* to join in. He'd always been sure that his knees and elbows would stick out, and his hands and feet would go all dangly, and he'd look like a complete and utter dork.

But now...

Anil didn't realise he'd got to his feet until he'd done it. It seemed to happen all by itself. He just found himself doing a high-five with Winsome and discovering that his legs were stomping about in time with the music.

He looked round, dazed, and found that the whole class was dancing. Jack was on the table doing a sort of moonwalk, and Winsome looked like something off an exercise video.

Even quiet little Emily was twirling round very fast on one pointed toe so that her skirt flared out round her. Anil had never seen anyone doing ballet to Sahara Ice Squirrel before, but it looked quite cool. But then, even *Rodney* looked quite cool. He was sleek and golden and appeared to be dancing a tango with Miss Broom.

*Weird,* Anil thought—and then suddenly discovered that he loved it. He loved it. He *loved* dancing.

The music from the beetle band had got even louder, and now there seemed to be words, as well. Yes, when Anil looked over at Miss Broom's desk he could see that the vocalist beetle (cockroach— of course, they were cockroaches) was holding a microphone.

The words had *not* been written by Sahara Ice Squirrel.

*Hey you guys, come listen to me,*
*You think you're great, but just you see,*
*A roach is cool, a roach is tough*
*You human dudes ain't good enough.*

And then the rest of the band joined in.

*Roach roach roach*
*The best life coach*
*Oh roach roach roach*
*That's us.*

*This is mad*, thought Anil, but his elbows were doing some really neat things and it was so brilliant he didn't want it to stop.

*Without my head I can live for a week,*
*I'm happy for a month with nothing to eat,*
*My brain is fine, my brain's not shoddy,*
*My brain is scattered all over my body.*

This time Anil found himself joining in with the chorus. *Roach roach roach*, he sang. He *never* sang.

If Winsome danced any faster she was going to take off.

*Four thousand lenses in my eye,*
*Look right and left, down low, up high,*
*I can hiss, I can fly, I don't need no protector—*
*My butt's got its own motion detector.*

*Roach roach roach*, Class Six sang, as they stepped and jumped and twirled.

*I've teeth in my belly and I've teeth in my head,*
*I eat glue and onions and anything dead,*
*My kids are never hungry, 'cos what they do*
*When times are hard is eat my poo.*

Anil suddenly realised that he was never going to forget any of this. Never. From now on he was going to be an expert on cockroaches.

Miss Broom and Rodney now seemed to be doing the dance called a rumba.

*We're older than humans, we're older than bees,*
*We were flying when the dinosaurs were at their*
     *mommies' knees,*
*Our mouths open sideways, and though we're*
     *born quite small*
*We blow ourselves up bigger like a new football.*

Anil's feet were stamping and stamping and there wasn't anything he could do to stop them.

*My blood is white, I've eighteen knees,*
*I'll give you plague 'cos I spread disease.*
*And now just one last word of warning—*
*My methane farts cause global warming.*

And then there was a huge crash, and everything stopped.

# CHAPTER FOURTEEN

Anil stood blinking across the classroom. The music had stopped and so had everyone's need to dance. Winsome was standing frozen with her hands in the air, and Emily was wobbling back down onto the soles of her feet.

Anil looked round some more. Slacker's huge body was on the carpet. He was panting as if he'd run a—well, actually, given that it was Slacker, he was panting as if he'd just *run*.

But Slacker didn't seem to be the source of the crash. Beyond him, at the front of the class, was a tangle of arms and legs. Anil could only tell who was there by the shoes. Two of the legs were wearing pointy-toed shoes with little curvy heels.

Miss Broom. That was Miss Broom.

And the other shoes were great things like paddle boats, only smellier.

Rodney. Of course, Miss Broom had been dancing with Rodney.

'What's happened?' demanded Slacker, trying to get up.

Serise took a cautious step forward. 'Miss Broom isn't dead, is she?' she asked, with only a tiny tinge of hope in her voice.

Emily squealed and jumped backwards.

Everyone looked at Winsome. Winsome was the sensible one: if anyone was going to know what to do, it would be Winsome.

Jack bent down and stared very closely at the jumble of arms and legs.

'Rodney's breathing,' he reported. 'At least, he's got puffs of smoke coming out of his ears.'

'How about Miss Broom?' quavered Emily.

'Oh, she seems to be dead all right. No, hang on, I think her nose is twitching.'

Serise frowned. 'Is that good? I mean, it isn't a death-twitch or anything, is it?'

'There's no such thing as a death-twitch,' said Anil. 'At least...there's not with humans. I don't think.'

'Hang on.' Slacker put up a hand up to one of his antennae. 'I seem to be receiving something. A sort of howling, like a police car.'

All of a sudden Rodney moved. He kicked out his leg so that one of his vast stinky shoes sailed off his foot, hit the ceiling, and ended up in the sink.

'Thank goodness!' said Winsome. 'Rodney! Rodney are you all right?'

Rodney got to his feet in a swift, elegant way which was as unlike Rodney as it could possibly be. He moved...he moved like a *leopard*.

Come to think of it, the brown spots on his face looked just like leopard spots, too.

Rodney cast a swift look round at the others.

'Well?' he said, in a voice that was almost a snarl.

Class Six smiled uncertainly at each other.

Behind Rodney, Miss Broom was twitching again. In fact she wasn't so much twitching as vibrating, faster and faster, until all Class Six could see was a blur.

And then she vanished. Completely. Just like that. One moment there was a full-sized teacher lying vibrating on the floor of the classroom, and the next there was nothing but empty space.

Several people screamed.

Rodney's staring eyes were like emeralds. His pupils had turned into big-cat slits.

And then he said the worst thing he could possibly have said.

'I'm hungry,' he said, and he licked his lips with a long pink tongue.

Emily squawked and tried to jump behind Jack, but as Jack did exactly the same thing at exactly the same time, all they did was bump into each other and fall over.

Everyone else began to back away. Rodney was flexing his fingers experimentally. They'd grown claws.

Serise looked round for a weapon and picked up a small plastic ruler.

'If only Miss Broom hadn't gone and vanished!' gasped Winsome. 'She could have saved us.'

Jack turned to her, frowning.

'I'll soon sort Rodney out,' he said in a dangerous sort of way—and Class Six saw to their horror that Jack's face had a strangely hairy look about it.

'Not him, too!' said Serise.

'It's all right, Jack!' said Winsome quickly. 'There's no need. I'm sure Rodney doesn't mean to hurt anyone. Do you, Rodney?'

'*Hurt* people?' Rodney echoed. He put his head on one side, as if considering the idea. Rodney had always been slow on the uptake. 'No, I don't want to hurt anyone—'

'Phew!' said half the class.

'—I just want to *eat* them,' Rodney went on, in his new growly voice. 'I just want to sink my teeth into their flesh and feel their blood spurting down my throat.'

Everyone became aware that Rodney was at the front of the classroom, so he was between Class Six and the door.

'Miss Broom!' called Winsome suddenly. 'Miss Broom, where are you? Because we could really do with a bit of help at the moment, please!'

Something made a swift fierce sound, but that was Rodney growling. He stepped quietly and heavily forward towards the rest of the class.

Jack moved forward to meet him.

'No!' said Anil, attaching himself to Jack's elbow.

'You don't want to fight Rodney. He's got claws and he thinks he's a leopard. And anyway, he's nuts!'

Jack looked up at Anil.

'But he's always been nuts,' he pointed out.

'Yes,' said Anil, 'but only in a harmless stupid sort of a way. The nits of doom have changed him. They've turned him vicious!'

Jack stopped for a moment, gazing at Anil with bright pink eyes.

'Well, you've got nits, too, just the same as him,' he said. 'My eyes have gone so they can see really tiny things, and I can see them in your hair.'

Class Six kept one eye on Rodney, but they couldn't resist shuffling closer to look at Anil's head.

'I can see the nits quite well against your black hair,' Jack went on. 'They're like tiny white rugby balls, but…hang on, they've got things inside them. They look a bit like squid and a bit like cheese graters, and they're all holding steering wheels.

Jack went to pick one of the nits out of Anil's hair, but it whizzed away from his fingers and dived down into one of the holes in Anil's skin where the hairs came out.

'It's gone inside your head,' said Jack.

'Erghhhh!' said Class Six. 'Errghhhhh! Errrghhhh! Errrrgghhhh!'

And then they all began scratching like mad.

'It's no good!' Emily was rubbing at her head until her hair stood on end. 'It's no good, I can feel them burrowing into my head! I can feel them driving through my brain! *What are we going to do?*'

Winsome was the only one standing still.

'Keep calm,' she said, determinedly. 'Panicking isn't going to help us. We need to keep calm and try to think what we can do.'

Anil had his hands clasped to his head.

'But we *can't* think what to do!' he cried. 'That's the point. The nits have got right into our brains and they're changing the way we're thinking.'

Emily freaked completely. 'Get them out, get them out!' she shrieked. 'I can't stand it!'

'Sshh!' commanded Slacker. 'Someone will hear you and come and see what's going on.'

Class Six wavered.

'Is it murder, do you think, making your teacher disappear into thin air?' asked Anil.

'Well, even if it is, it wasn't me!' said Serise. '*I* didn't touch her!'

'It was all of us,' said Winsome, very worried. 'I wonder if it's a crime to turn someone into a leopard?'

'But Rodney might be something else by the time the police get here,' said Slacker, hopefully. 'He might be something really friendly and nice, like a… hamster.'

Serise snorted.

'There is *no way* Rodney could possibly end up being anything at all like a hamster,' she said. 'A ten-ton gorilla, possibly, but—'

'Don't even think about it!' said Anil, shuddering.

Jack suddenly sat down.

'I hate to mention this,' he said, 'but talking of gorillas, I've got this terrible craving for bananas. And my armpits are really itchy, as well. And—' He squinted down inside his shirt. 'Yes, I thought so. I've got black hair sprouting out all over my chest.'

Everyone shuffled away from Jack, remembered about Rodney, and shuffled back again.

'It might not mean I'm going to be a gorilla, though,' said Jack, thoughtfully. 'I might just be turning into a chimpanzee. I wouldn't mind that so much.'

'But what should we do? ' asked Serise. 'Do we call for help and get taken to prison for murdering our teacher, or do we let one of us be eaten by a leopard?'

'Bags not me to be eaten,' said Anil, quickly. 'I'm too bony. Rodney might eat me and still be hungry. It'd be much better to let him eat someone fatter. Hey,' he went on, brightening, 'we could say he ate Miss Broom, too!'

'Good thinking,' said Serise, who was as skinny as a broomstick herself.

Slacker Punchkin began shaking his head. 'Well, I think that's a totally rubbish—' Then he twitched, and his antennae started to flash alternate red and green.

Slacker put a meaty hand up to one of them. 'Hang on,' he said. 'I think I'm getting a new radio station.'

There was a blood-curdling snarl behind them and everyone leapt several centimetres into the air. Rodney was on all fours, now. He seemed to have grown lots of new sharp teeth. A line of glistening spit was hanging down to the floor from one of them.

Slacker was pushing his front teeth into his gums one by one.

'I can hear wailing,' he reported.

'You're picking up my brain waves,' quavered Emily, who was as pale and shivery as a blancmange in an earthquake.

'Or mine,' admitted Winsome. 'I keep trying to think what to do, but my head's just full of wailing.'

Class Six looked at each other.

'Even Rodney looks as if he can hear it,' said Anil, because Rodney was batting at his ear with a hand which was halfway to being a paw.

Slacker frowned. He was screwing up his face as if he was listening really carefully.

'Everyone shut up a minute,' he said. 'I think I nearly got it in tune just then. I think... Hang on!' He switched to twisting his chin, and began to look more confident.

'That's it,' he said. 'It's on FM, not digital. It's someone saying something.'

Jack began to twist his chin, too. 'You're right. It's a voice, a long way away. I think it's saying...'

'What?' said everyone. 'What's it saying?'

Jack looked round at them all.

*'Ball the chits,'* he said.

# CHAPTER FIFTEEN

Serise rolled her eyes.

'Oh you idiot!' she said. 'You moron! You utter and complete cretin! Just what is *ball the chits* supposed to mean?'

'Well,' said Jack, 'I suppose we have to find the... er...chits, and then, er...'

'Give me strength!' said Serise, despairingly.

'Where's my dictionary?' asked Winsome. She got it from her drawer and flicked urgently through the pages. 'Chit... chit... no, it's not here. It goes straight from chisel to chivalry.'

Slacker put his hand thoughtfully to his chin— and then suddenly stood up straight.

'That's it!' he said. 'I've just accidentally tuned the station in properly. Jack heard it wrong. That wasn't *ball the chits* we picked up on our antennae, that was *ball the NITS!*'

'*Ball the nits!*' proclaimed Jack. 'Hurray! We've got it! Er…how can anyone ball a nit?'

Rodney was almost completely a leopard now. He was crouching on the floor by Miss Broom's desk, warm and velvet-furred and dangerous. Only his glowing antennae, and the fact that he was wearing trousers and an orange sweatshirt, gave away the fact that he was not a real leopard.

Slacker put his hand up to his chin again.

'I can still hear it,' he said. '*Ball the nits.* Again and again. At least, I think…'

Rodney's eyes were glowing like the fires at the centre of the earth.

He stretched out a long arm, and his muscles moved smoothly under his beautiful fur. Each heavy paw looked as if it could knock someone's head off.

Class Six had put all the tables between them and Rodney, but it was no use. Rodney crouched for a moment, with only the twitching of the black tips of his ears to show that he had not been turned to stone—and then he sprang.

They all tried to get out of the way, but there were twenty-nine of them and only a small space behind the tables. The ones at the back fell over chair legs, and the rest fell over them.

The leopard would have landed in the middle of the whole struggling panicking mass of children if it hadn't been for his trousers. Rodney's waistband got caught up round a table leg and he ended up crashing down with a great snarling and cracking of table tops and fluttering of pieces of paper.

Nearly everyone was too busy trying to disentangle their arms and legs from everybody else's to think about anything but GETTING AWAY FROM THE LEOPARD, but Slacker had bumped his chin on Anil's head and he was almost too dazed to move.

'Ball the chits,' he muttered, blearily. 'Ball the nits...'

He suddenly sat up straight. And then he said 'Nits!' in a sharp, loud voice.

Then he said it again, even louder. '*Nits!*'

'Oh flip, now Slacker's gone bonkers,' said Anil, crawling under one of the least smashed of the tables. 'What's he keep calling out *nits* for?'

Winsome frowned.

'Calling...' she began, and then her eyes flashed with realisation. 'That's what it was. Not *ball the nits,* it was *call the nits*!' She turned to the rest of the class. 'Quick!' she shouted. 'It's our only chance. Call the nits!'

Class Six didn't waste any time arguing. There was a big leopard loose in the classroom, and it had nearly managed to kick its way out of its trousers.

'Nits!' they called.

'NITS!!' they bellowed.

## 'NITS!!!'

Jack felt it first—a sharp tickle behind his ear. Then Winsome's elbow twitched sharply for no reason at all. Serise's foot lifted itself up and began waggling about as if she were trying to kick her shoe off.

Suddenly all the class were twitching and shivering as strange wiggly feelings ran through them from their toes to their belly buttons and right up to the ends of their eyelashes.

The Rodney-leopard gave a great angry snarl, but then there was a *crack!* as if the floor had split in two, and a brilliant flash which meant that all anyone could see for several seconds were floaty orange blobs.

When the blobs faded, Class Six saw that a big-bosomed figure with sandy hair had appeared at the front of the classroom.

Miss Broom looked round the classroom at the heap of bewildered children, and all the wrecked tables and chairs.

'Good gracious,' she said. 'Great moonbeams above.'

And she put her hands behind her ears and flipped them three times.

At once all the splinters and odd pieces of wood from the tables and chairs jumped about, did various somersaults, and slotted themselves neatly back together again. Anil had to duck pretty sharply to avoid being bashed on the ear by a chair back, but in less than a minute Class Six found themselves somewhere that looked like a classroom again, and not like the scene of an earthquake with a bit of car-crash thrown in.

'And now,' said Miss Broom, turning to Class Six, 'what about all of *you*?'

And Class Six, terrified, knew that any moment now a real live genuine witch was going to find out...

'Great unicycling unicorns!' said Miss Broom, as a snarl alerted her to the fact that there was a half-boy half-leopard crouching on the floor. 'I know that vacant look and that slack jaw. Why, it's Rodney, isn't it?'

No one answered. Miss Broom cast a sharp glance round the room.

'Yes, it's Rodney turned into a leopard,' Miss Broom went on. 'How odd. And inconvenient. And dangerous.'

She glanced round again, and everyone hurriedly looked away, trying to make themselves invisible again.

It didn't work, of course. Class Six had been getting less invisible ever since the day they were born, and now, adorned with fluorescent antennae, fur and wobbly trunks, they would have stood out at a Science Fiction convention.

'Great icicles of Snark,' said Miss Broom. 'How utterly terrible. I'd no idea what a simple nit infestation could do to human children. I mean, your symptoms are bad enough, but those witch-nits have set up such nasty brain-waves in your poor human heads that they actually sent me most of the way to Timbuktu. You've no idea what a shock it was for me to find myself in the Sahara desert. I'm not sure the camels will ever get over the surprise.'

Miss Broom looked round at them all again.

'This is highly dangerous,' she said.

'Yes!' said Emily. 'Rodney wants to eat us!'

'I can see that,' said Miss Broom. 'But that's not the worst of it. Now, all of you, listen to me. A witch-nit infestation obviously does all sorts of strange things to humans.'

'It gives you green toes,' said Anil.

'And purple fluff in your belly button,' said Slacker Punchkin.

'And even worse, they seem to make your veins clog up so in the end they will stop working altogether,' finished up Miss Broom, sadly.

Everyone gasped.

'But that would kill us!' said Winsome, aghast.

'They *are* nits of doom!' said Anil.

'I don't want to die,' Emily said, very quickly. 'I don't want to die! I want to grow up and wear high heels and worry if my handbag's the right shape!'

'Handbags?' echoed Serise, outraged. 'Blow handbags! This is just *so* unfair. This means I'll never get to start a weapons factory or become president of the universe.'

Winsome nodded sadly.

'Or be a doctor,' she said.

'Or drive a car!'

'Or be a model!'

'Or have my own horse!'

'Or a restaurant!'

'Or a huge train lay-out!'

Miss Broom shook her head sorrowfully.

'I suppose I must have left the cupboard door unlocked,' she said. 'And someone tried my hat on. That must have been Rodney, mustn't it, as he's the most changed.'

Jack spoke up. 'Will we *all* turn into animals first?'

'My dear Class Six,' said Miss Broom. 'Turn into animals? Die all over the place? Great turnips of Tresco, I hope not! But you must all be very brave and clever. The really hugely important thing is that you *mustn't scratch*. You see, all the nits have come out of your pores, now you've called them, and they're sitting on your skin. But if you scratch or move suddenly you'll frighten them and they'll go back in and refuse to come out again. So *don't scratch*. All right?'

At once Class Six's skins begin to shiver and itch.

And itch and itch and itch.

Class Six clenched their fists and screwed up their faces and tried as hard as they could not to scratch, even though they had little tickles and prickles and creepy feelings as if spiders were running about all over them.

'I've just got to scratch,' said Jack desperately.

'Don't!' said Winsome.

'I must!' said Anil. 'I feel as if I've got earwigs in my ears.'

'Don't!' said Winsome.

'It's no good,' gasped Serise. 'We're all going to die!'

'I can't stand it!' squeaked Emily. 'I've got to scratch, I've got to—'

'Great bananas of Bongo!' exclaimed Miss Broom. 'My dear Class Six, what am I?'

Class Six blinked at her.

'Winsome,' Miss Broom said. 'You tell them. What am I?'

Winsome frowned with concentration, holding her hands together to stop herself scratching. 'You're a…a…a…*ditch*, Miss Broom.'

Miss Broom laughed a strange mad laugh that raised the fur on the back of all their necks.

'Nearly right,' she said. 'I'm a *witch*. That's what I am, a witch, a witch, a WITCH! That means, amongst other things, that I'm the best teacher in the world. I can take you down to the centre of the earth to see the continents floating along on their oceans of molten rock. I can take you up in an invisible balloon to watch the comets screaming through the sky. I can show you the secrets of the gnome-finch, the way you make ear wax, and how the hippo cleans its teeth.'

Anil sighed and sat down on his hands.

'That all sounds so brilliant,' he said longingly. 'I wish...I do wish I *wasn't* going to die. I'd love to learn all that stuff.'

'You haven't got time just to tell us about the ear wax, have you?' asked Winsome wistfully.

'I'm afraid not,' said Miss Broom. 'Because this is really much too serious. In fact, I think you had all better sit at your tables.'

Numbly, Class Six did as they were told.

'Now,' said Miss Broom sweetly.

And she began to dance.

It was an old-fashioned sort of dance. It looked the sort of thing a cannibal might do round a cauldron; or perhaps like the dance a bear might do who was celebrating finding an enormous hive full of honey.

Class Six watched her, and even though Miss Broom looked really funny they didn't feel like laughing at all.

'*Look!*' shouted Serise.

There was a thing like a tiny white rugby ball flying through the air towards the front of the classroom.

'There's another one!' cried Slacker.

They were everywhere now, a whole blizzard of tiny white capsules, streaming through the air and heading for...

Miss Broom shivered happily and patted gently at her springy sandy hair.

'Lovely,' she murmured, as Class Six gaped in horror. 'Beautiful. There's nothing like a community of nice active witch-nits charging round one's veins to perk up one's magic. But only if one is a witch, it seems. Otherwise I'm afraid these nits really are agents of doom.'

There was a kerfuffle at the front of the classroom and Rodney's head and pink bare shoulders popped up behind Miss Broom's desk. He gazed round at everyone, screamed, and ducked down again.

Slacker put up a huge hand to feel for his antennae. They weren't there.

'I can't pick up Foodie FM any more,' he said. 'Blow it! There was going to be a recipe for blackberry and ginger crumble on the half hour.'

'My arms have got shorter,' whispered Jack, as if he could hardly believe it.

'And my trunk,' said someone.

'And my chest isn't hairy any more.'

'But of course,' said Miss Broom. 'Well, I couldn't let my whole class drop dead, could I? People would have noticed. Your parents might have been upset. Complained, even. Especially if you'd all turned into leopards first.'

'So do you mean...we're cured?' asked Winsome, hardly able to believe it.

'Of course!' said Miss Broom. 'Well, you're back to normal, anyway. Yes, just as you were before, except for being a little older and possibly just a tiny bit wiser. And as for the nits, snacking on your odd non-witchy brainwaves has perked them up no end. Yes, I can feel them fizzing away inside my brain like sherbet.'

'You mean you've got all our nits *on your own head*?' Serise said.

'That's right. They're a great help. I'm not sure what I'd do without them. Probably be rather evil, I should imagine.'

Class Six looked at each other.

'So...*aren't* you evil, then, Miss Broom?' asked Anil, at last, politely.

'I mean, we know you've been really nice so far,' said Winsome. 'Teaching us our tables and all that. And PE was fantastic. But...'

Miss Broom seemed rather offended. 'Really!' she said. 'Do I *look* evil?'

Class Six looked at each other some more.

'Not really,' said Winsome at last.

'Not *really*?'

'It's just that the things we see in your eyes are a bit frightening sometimes,' explained Anil. 'You know, all those ruined temples and pterodactyls and screaming ghosts and stuff.'

'And the skeletons,' said someone, feelingly.

Miss Broom put her hands up to her face in dismay. 'Skeletons?' she echoed.

'And hands with huge claws,' said Emily. 'Wearing black nail varnish.'

Miss Broom clutched at her sandy hair in horror.

'Oh *no!*' she said. 'That's just *terrible*! Oh my dears, you poor things. Just a moment, will you?'

She turned her back on the class, and seemed to be trying to take her eyes out.

'There!' she said, turning back. 'Better?'

Class Six stared at Miss Broom's eyes. They could still clearly see the pictures floating across them.

'Silver flying horses,' said Emily, in wonder.

'And pink teddy bears,' said Serise, in some distaste. 'Yuk, where on earth did they get those tartan waistcoats from?'

Miss Broom heaved a sigh of relief.

'Thank heavens for that,' she said. 'You know, I *thought* I wasn't seeing as well as I should have been. Just think, I must have been wearing my contact

124

lenses inside out for a whole week. Ooh yes, I can see much better now.'

Behind her Rodney stood up. He was fully clothed and not even slightly a leopard. He walked carefully round Miss Broom's desk and back to his seat.

Class Six sighed. The sight of those teddy bears had made them feel much calmer. Happier, too. As if having a witch for a teacher might be quite fun. Incredible fun.

Absolutely *stupendous* fun.

'Hey, Rodney,' said Slacker Punchkin, as Rodney settled himself down. 'I bet you've changed your mind now.'

'What about?' asked Rodney.

'About Miss Broom. About what she is.'

'Changed my mind?' said Rodney.

'Yes,' said Serise. 'You were wrong, weren't you?'

Rodney shrugged.

'So go on, then, admit it,' said Anil. 'Tell us. Tell us what Miss Broom is!'

Rodney looked round at the rest of the class, puzzled.

'Miss Broom? What she is?' he asked. 'Well, she's...'

'Yes?' said Anil.

'She's...'

'Yes?' said Jack.

'She's...'

'*Yes?*' said everybody.

'She's a teacher,' said Rodney, still very puzzled.

Class Six couldn't believe it.

'You idiot!' shouted Serise. 'Five minutes ago you were a leopard!'

'Yesterday you were flying round the school hall!' yelped Anil.

'Oh, those were just dreams,' said Rodney. 'I think I must have eaten too much cheese or something.'

Class Six clutched at their nit-free hair in exasperation.

'It wasn't a dream!' they all shouted. 'It was *real*!'

Rodney shook his head.

'That's impossible,' he said, patiently.

'NO IT'S NOT!' Class Six howled.

'But how could it possibly be true?' asked Rodney, bewildered.

Class Six took in a deep breath and tried one last time to get the message into Rodney's big thick skull.

'It's true,' they shouted, 'because Miss Broom is a **WIBBLE!**'